ANOTHER Face-Off

A WILDCATTERS HOCKEY BOOK

BOOK 5

ALEXA PADGETT

For Danielle.

*You have been such an amazing boon to my career,
and I cannot thank you enough!*

CHAPTER 1
Paxton

I sat up in bed, and my head felt heavy in my hands—and not just because of the hangover from last night's pity-party after I attended Naomi and Adam's baby shower.

My teammate and mentor, Lennon Cruz, appeared in my doorway, as if conjured by magic.

"You stayed here?" I croaked.

I had a large house—four bedrooms, a media room, home gym—in the same neighborhood as a few of the other Wildcatters players. I kept two of the additional bedrooms stocked for a needy teammate or friend, but half the house sat unused. Sad.

"Yeah, man. Was worried about you," Cruz said.

If I hadn't broken up with Hana, like a damn fool, three years ago, maybe we'd have a kid in one of those unused rooms. My headache bloomed into a painful thrum as I conjured the sound of laughter bouncing off the walls.

"Thanks," I told him. I owed Cruz about twenty favors.

"OJ and painkillers on the nightstand. Down 'em and hop in the shower."

"Why?" I asked.

He raised an eyebrow. "We're going to California."

"W-*what?*"

"Because you can't keep putting this off."

"What?" I asked, narrowing my eyes.

"Hana."

"What do you know about Hana?"

"You mean besides the sob-fest version from last night?"

"I *cried* about her?" My dry eyes disliked me widening them, but I was too shocked to control the reaction.

"On my shoulder." Cruz patted his thick pec. "And not just about her—about your parents after I wondered why you were spending the holidays alone."

"I wasn't alone; I went with you to your family's Thanksgiving." Where I'd eaten the best tamales ever. Mama Cruz might be a tall, languid woman, but she turned into a three-star general in her kitchen.

"Here's the name of the startup Hana's working for." Cruz let the paper flutter to my nightstand next to the glass of juice and pills.

"You know where she's working? That seems like…stalking."

Cruz scoffed. "Like I'd ever stalk a woman."

"So then how did you get the information in like, seven hours?"

"We'll talk about that on the plane."

"No," I said. "We'll talk about it now."

He raised an eyebrow. "You told me the story about Hana on your birthday."

"I did? That was months ago!"

"Nearly a year now. You were all pitiful after seeing Maxim with Ida Jane."

That I didn't remember, probably because I'd been plastered. But I did know how Maxim looked at his wife, and each time

I saw that devotion in his eyes and her soft smile back, I was reminded of Hana.

Cruz had taken care of me that night, too, and not said anything to the guys about it, for which I was thankful. I still wasn't ready to discuss Hana with the team.

"Last night was simply the callback to that, which told me you still care too much to let go of the hope of a future with her."

He wasn't wrong. And I was positive Hana was my soulmate, but that didn't change the hurt I'd caused her. I closed my eyes and swallowed, grimacing at the terrible taste in my mouth.

"Ass out of bed, Naese. You only have an hour-fifty to pack for our next game and get yourself showered."

"Why?" I croaked. I opened my aching eyes and looked at him.

His expression seemed to soften beneath that thick beard. "You need to talk to your girl. Get up," he said again. "We really should leave in an hour and a half. I'm not going to let you mess up this meet-and-greet I worked hard to put together."

"I…" I shut my mouth.

Last night's baby shower had caused a resurgence of my disgust at walking away from Hana, the love of my life. It was a constant battle now to swallow my disappointment in myself. At least I'd made some better choices since coming to Houston, and I was long past the point where casual relationships filled the void of loneliness I'd ripped into my soul when I told Hana we were through.

I hadn't once felt a connection to another woman like the bond I'd shared with Hana. So, I'd simply become less and less satisfied with my dating life and my hockey career. For the first time ever, I was unsure how to correct the problems. Normally, I'd call my dad and get advice from him, but he'd been the one to push me to end things with Hana. In fact, my parents had nailed our coffin shut and thrown it out to sea when my father told me I had to choose between my family and career or the woman who was holding me back.

I'd listened to him, but I'd come to hate him for his words.

I was furious—with my father, especially—*so* angry that I wasn't sure I'd ever forgive either of my parents. But I shouldered the blame for not calling Hana back a few days later after she'd left me a message.

If I had…

If I had, maybe she'd be here with me in this bed, and I'd be happy. I could barely remember what that felt like anymore. Even the camaraderie of my teammates failed to chip away the coldness that seemed to surround my soul.

"Why?" I asked again, the rest of the words choked off because my throat ached. My response to Cruz was embarrassing. He'd caught me while I was down, and I hated getting emotional.

"You don't have to keep beating yourself up over a mistake you made years ago," he said, his murderous resting face softening…a little. Cruz would always look like he was going to kill someone. It was part of his charm—that and his brutal checks and punches on the ice.

I loved the guy. In fact, we all adored Cruz.

"From what you said last night, your father also bears some blame," he noted. "You admitted to the screw up, and now it's time to take back control. She may not want you, and you'll have to deal with that, but at least you can get out of being stuck."

I was sick of pretending I was okay—I wasn't. I missed Hana. I screwed my eyes tightly shut.

I miss her terribly.

My hands fisted, and anger pumped through me—hot, heady, and dangerous if I didn't find a proper outlet. I didn't want to lash out at my friends...or Hana.

No, this was a rush I should unleash in practices, maybe a game.

I swallowed down my initial reaction. My next step was to fix the situation with Hana. I was determined to wash off last night's overindulgence and then move on to my parents' lies. The only way to get Hana back was to talk to her.

I turned on the taps in my shower and stripped off the boxer briefs and T-shirt I'd slept in. I was a professional hockey player with multiple years in the league. I played for one of the best teams because Coach had traded for me partway through my first season. To most people, I seemed to have it all.

Professionally, I did. But I noted how happy Coach was with his wife, Paloma. Adam and Naomi were all lovey-dovey, as were Cormac and Keelie, and now the mighty Maxim Dolov and his tiny obsession, Ida Jane.

Even notorious ladies' man Luka Stol had settled into familial bliss, that fucking asshole. And here I was, still chasing the thing I'd always wanted—and had let slip through my fingers.

Cruz pounded on my bathroom door. "Thirty minutes till we gotta leave!"

"I'll be ready," I called. I hissed as I stepped into the stall, but the lure of seeing Hana again kept me rooted in the space.

Hana. We'd known each other practically our whole lives. Her family had moved in down the street right before second grade. Hana and her older brother, Aiki, had arrived just days before we started classes. I'd met them in the vacant lot between our houses. Aiki was loud and fun—a rough-and-tumble boy who didn't mind getting dirty, or in trouble.

But Hana was quiet. Many people considered her shy. She wasn't, though, not once you got to know her. She just assessed a situation before stepping into it, an essential part of her personality, just like hockey was to me.

Aiki and I had gotten on well because we both liked sports and running around, but it was Hana that drew me closer, and I'd spent more of my time with her by late elementary school.

There had never even been even the idea of another woman for me. Hana and I had started dating our sophomore year of high school. Her mother was traditional in her values and culture, and that meant Hana and I had less freedom to spend time together than before we'd made our relationship official.

I soaped my body, staring down at the drain, watching the suds build up there.

But I'd told her I would never hide how much I cared for her, how proud I was that she wanted me, too.

That was all true.

Until I blew it up. I groaned, shoving the heels of my hands into my eyes as I remembered that conversation and the painful reality of the aftermath.

"*You don't need to come to the draft,*" I'd said, shifting my weight, my father's words spinning through my head.

"*Of course I'm going to be there,*" Hana said, smiling. Her dark eyes had shone bright with pride and excitement. "*I need to show the world how proud I am of my man.*" She'd run her palms down my chest, and a warm tingle had lit me up even as my heart pounded.

"*But that's just it,*" I'd blurted.

She'd pulled back, confusion marring her soft white brow. "*What's it?*"

"*I'm not your man.*"

Her eyes had widened as my heart dropped not just to my feet but seemingly out of my body. I'd done it. I'd started the process of breaking up with the only girl I'd ever dated. The only woman I'd loved.

And I'd watched her face pale, her eyes widen. Hana rarely showed great emotion with anyone, so I wasn't surprised when she'd bowed her head to hide the tears forming in her eyes. I knew they were there, though, because my eyes were filled, too.

"*You have another semester of college,*" I'd told her, my words pouring out of me faster, and faster. "*And I'm going to some other city—maybe across the country…*"

"*I'll go with you—*"

"*No, Hana. I know how important your studies are to you. You worked so hard to get into a top-tier school. You shouldn't have to give up that diploma for me.*"

She'd raised her head then, the fire in her eyes battling with the wet streaks down her cheeks. "*So instead you're going to break up with me. Just…dump me because I don't fit in easily to your new life?*"

I'd bitten my cheek, staring at her for a long moment. Myriad thoughts had rushed through my head, mostly my father's words. *"Too young... Never even looked at another woman... Can't know this relationship is what you want..."*

He'd made sense, hadn't he? *"There are going to be so many girls and parties,"* I'd tried to explain. *"There's no way I could—"*

"Be very careful what you say next, Pax," Hana had said, her voice soft, yet filled with a layer of steel I rarely heard from her.

"W-what do you mean?" I'd asked.

"It sounds like you're saying these other women will tempt you, and you don't have the discipline to stay faithful," Hana replied, her lovely amber-colored eyes narrowed to slits.

"I—no, that's not what I mean."

Was it? Had my dad been telling me I didn't have the willpower? I frowned. I loved Hana. I'd been faithful to this point. Why wouldn't I continue to be faithful?

I'd shaken my head, confusion beating at my skull.

"Then what do you mean?" Hana had asked.

"That...that... It's just too hard to keep us going when you're in Boston, and I'm somewhere else."

Hana had studied me a moment, and her face slowly turned into a mask—an expression I most often saw when she was around her mother. For whatever reason, Hana and Mrs. Sato didn't get along well. Hana had never explained why, though I'd asked numerous times.

My throat had closed as panic gripped me. My dad had said I was doing the right thing, setting her free, trying to make sure Hana had the opportunities to meet her full potential.

This was right, wasn't it? I was being the bigger person. So why did I feel so small? So miserable.

"*You know what?*" Hana had said.

"*What?*"

"*You're just like everyone else in my life.*" With that she'd turned and walked away, her shoulders hunched.

I'd spent a sleepless night, and unable to handle the divide between us, I'd gone over to Hana's house early the next morning. I'd needed to talk to her and make sure she knew how much I cared for her…

When the door had opened, Mrs. Sato stood there, smiling brightly. Her face was more animated than I'd ever seen it. "*You did the right thing.*"

"*It doesn't feel right,*" I muttered. "*In fact, I don't think I can—*"

"*You can,*" she snapped. "*You will. It's for Hana's future. You should never have had the opportunity to disrupt her path.*"

For the first time in that moment, I saw the tyrant Hana had rarely mentioned but clearly knew well. Mrs. Sato didn't have Hana's best interest at heart. I'd realized the older woman was creating a future for her daughter that she wanted for herself. One that didn't—and had never—included me.

And the off-kilter feeling had grown. I *had* to see Hana; I'd explain—

"*You will not see her,*" Mrs. Sato had countered.

And I'd realized I'd spoken aloud. Straightening my shoulders and lifting my chin, I'd stared into her eyes. "*I love your daughter.*"

She'd scoffed. "*If you did, you wouldn't have been so quick to listen to your father.*"

How had *she* known about that? Had my dad and Mrs. Sato talked about Hana and me, decided our future? I'd felt duped. No, this couldn't stand. I'd stepped back and looked up at the second-story window in Hana's bedroom.

"*What good is love?*" Mrs. Sato had sneered. "*It doesn't offer security or respectability. My daughter deserves better than mere love. Go.*" She'd waved me off. "*You aren't welcome here again.*"

I'd stumbled back, shocked as Mrs. Sato shut the door with a hard click, nearly popping me in the nose. As I'd turned in a circle, unsure what to do, Aiki had slunk around the side of the house, a smirk on his face.

We hadn't gotten along so well since I'd started dating Hana. Actually, we hadn't gotten along since I'd grown seven inches taller than him in the eighth grade. But he was my only hope.

"*Aiki, you know how I feel about Hana,*" I'd started. "*This… it… My dad, your mom—it's wrong. You gotta help me, man.*"

Aiki's smirk had bloomed into a full smile. "*No, actually, I don't. You lost your chance.*" He'd practically crowed the words.

I'd tried to get around him, but he blocked me. Within a moment, I'd realized he was ready to use all his pent-up anger and aggression against me. I couldn't get to her now. I'd pulled out my phone.

Aiki had snatched it from me. "*You had your chance, and you threw it—and her—away,*" he'd called back over his shoulder. "*Don't ever forget that.*"

I'd stood there, stunned for a moment before I took off after him. But I was too late. He'd pelted around the corner and out of sight.

Mrs. Sato had opened the door and yelled, "*She's not here, anyway!*" Then she'd slammed the door shut again.

After I'd moped around outside, then inside for the next several hours, my father had suggested we leave that day for the draft. After we arrived, my friend from the Junior Nationals team, Davis, had tried to cheer me up with lots of sexy girls, but I wasn't that interested in them—or in having a good time—until I'd gotten a text message from Hana the next day on the new phone my father had gotten me:

Hana: I never want to talk to you again.

After reading that, I decided those other women looked pretty nice after all, and I leaned hard into the partying. But it always left me empty, even more so after my first-choice coach, Silas Whittaker, had told me the Wildcatters were passing on me because of my surprising and wild behavior.

Instead of reining it in, even then I'd leaned into it more, hoping the other women would fill the hole of Hana's absence. They hadn't.

"Move your ass, Naese!" Cruz bellowed through the door.

I'd *finally* figured out that Hana hadn't sent that text message. It had taken me a long time—too long—to realize my father had given me a new phone with a new number. A number Hana wouldn't have.

Maybe if I'd returned home after that first season, I would have been able to talk to her. But I hadn't. I'd been too angry at my father for his part in breaking my—and her—heart. And I couldn't bear to look down the street and see her house, remembering all our shared moments.

So instead of returning home, I'd bought a house in Houston after I was traded mid-season. I'd hoped to show management I intended to put down roots. I still had lots of women around because I enjoyed their company, and I liked the idea of Hana being jealous, but I couldn't stomach the idea of building a relationship with any of them.

For a while, only Cruz knew those women were a front, that my party-boy persona hid the turbulent disappointment of my youthful dreams. Cruz never told a soul, not even Coach, though I was pretty certain Silas Whittaker had figured me out before he offered my agent the trade deal—that's probably *why* he'd been willing to talk to my agent about a trade. The man left little to chance, and he had an amazing team to show for it.

I turned off the water, dried myself, and dressed in record time. I threw some extra clothes into my bag to accommodate the additional days I'd be gone. Then I gathered that and the garment bag that held my suits for the road trip, thankful I always re-packed my bag while I was cleaning out the dirty items.

I met Cruz at the door that led from my kitchen out through a mud room and into the garage. He looked me up and down critically. "You ready for this?"

"No, but I have to face it—face her," I said. "Try to explain, if she'll let me."

He grunted as we threw our bags into the backseat of his truck. "Yeah, that's the key: if she'll let you. But it's worth the shot, and I can't stand your moping anymore."

We spent the next few hours of travel—to the airport, on the flight, after we had the rental car—trying to come up with a plan that would allow me to get Hana to believe my crazy story. I still couldn't believe it was the truth.

"Doubt any of this is going to work," Cruz muttered as he pulled our car to a stop at the campus where Hana worked. He looked me up and down. "Good luck. I hope she's more forgiving than most people."

I scowled. "That's a terrible pep talk. This was your idea!"

"Not here to talk you up, brother." He cast me a side-eye. "I'm here for when it doesn't work."

Well, fuck.

CHAPTER 2
Hana

I stared out the window, wishing I hadn't agreed to run this round of data. It was the time I'd normally be gathering my things to go, and I was tired.

I'd been tired for so long, I wasn't sure I remembered what energetic or happy felt like. At first, I'd chalked my exhaustion up to healing, and that was at least partly true. But the fatigue should have passed by now. It hadn't, and I was starting to think it never would.

I thought everything had fallen apart when Paxton broke up with me, but the real slump had hit when I'd miscarried our child later that week. It had been raining then, and I'd hated the rain ever since.

I hadn't known I was pregnant, so the nurse had told me I couldn't really miss the baby.

I'd abhorred that nurse with every fiber of my being from that moment until I left the hospital. She knew it, too, and had tried to avoid my room. When she'd come in to check my vitals, she'd kept her eyes averted.

For a while, my rage toward her kept me going. But eventually, even hate gives out. Then I was left with grief and loneliness, along with a painful road to recovery.

"I preferred the hate," I muttered to myself. But even as I said it, I knew it wasn't true. I just preferred not feeling empty and sad.

I sighed, tracing the raindrop's slide down the window before pulling my attention back to the computer. I didn't want to think about Paxton. I never did, but he still crept up on me—an insidious need I couldn't shake. I intended to hate him for that, too. The data was mostly analyzed now. Only another hour, maybe two. Then I could crawl into bed…and toss and turn restlessly.

I sighed. I needed to move past this funk, but I didn't know how.

Jeremy's hands settled on my neck and began to massage the knots there. "You're awfully tense," he whispered in my ear.

"I know." I didn't enjoy his caresses nor the ear-whispering, which tickled my sensitive skin.

"Is it because of the simulation we're going to run tomorrow?" he asked. "You know it's stellar work. You always blow me away, Han. I can't believe such a beautiful package houses such a brilliant mind." He kissed my cheek.

I bit back a grimace. I hadn't invited his touch. I just hadn't rejected it either. And I should have, because I didn't like him touching me. I didn't like much in the way of physical contact these days, not after the months of being poked and prodded by medical professionals.

"Please. Not now, Jeremy."

"How about later?"

"I'm not feeling great."

"Is this because of your leg?"

I nodded. But my leg, which often hurt, wasn't the issue right now. My lack of interest in touch was much more relevant, but I was too worn out to bring it up, especially with Jeremy. He had a habit of steamrolling my concerns, and I couldn't allow that—not now that he'd made it clear he wanted intimacy.

The mere thought made my stomach cramp and turn.

Soon Jeremy would figure out that I was throwing excuses to keep from taking him to my home and my bed. I just didn't want him—not as my lover or my partner, not even as my boss.

But he'd been one of the few people interested in me after I recovered enough from multiple surgeries to seek a job. I'd managed to complete my degree from my hospital bed, the only blessing being that the boredom—and the inability to move—had helped me whiz through more classes than I'd been able to take in person.

I should've been more thankful for everything Jeremy had done for me. It was a lot. Jeremy Dorring was brilliant and ambitious. He'd already started a company and had a multimillion-dollar investment in his project that would make it easier for humans on Earth to ship materials to the moon. The work was engaging, cutting edge. But brilliance and an attractive exterior did *nothing* for me these days. I traced another raindrop. I just wanted…*what?*

The answer came quickly. I wanted to feel happy. Alive.

"Well, then, why don't I get you a cup of tea? That'll be soothing. Green, right?"

I managed not to roll my eyes. Green tea wouldn't soothe my leg. Worse, I hated green tea. It was bitter, my mother's favorite drink. Still, I smiled and nodded, mainly because I wanted Jeremy to go away.

How unfair of me... But the need to be alone expanded, pressing on my nerve endings, making me want to scream.

Jeremy's footsteps drifted down the hall toward the community break room. I sighed in relief. I wasn't sure how I was going to get through the rest of this day, let alone the rest of the year—or next year. I shut my eyes and breathed deeply, slowly, as I tried to ease the tension in my shoulders and neck.

I didn't want to spend my life working in this world. I didn't care about the physics or money related to a moon ladder. I just, I wanted—

"Hey, man. How are you? Have you seen Hana Sato?"

I gasped as I leaped to my feet, then stumbled as my brace dug into the flesh of my thigh. I shifted my balance because that leg couldn't bear the weight without proper support. No! No, no, *no*.

I slipped my hands under my skirt and shifted the metal that kept the sides stiff, repositioning it so the cloth settled against my skin as it was supposed to. But thanks to my sudden movement, my leg began to ache.

"Who's asking?" Jeremy's tone was belligerent.

"We're friends. Old friends. I grew up a couple of houses from her. I really need to get in touch with her now. It's important."

No, we weren't friends. We were lovers, soulmates, but now—for the last three years—we were *nothing*.

But Jeremy must have decided Pax was telling the truth, because he said, "Lab Two, on the left."

Before I could decide what to do, Pax was there, filling up the doorway, bigger and more beautiful than I remembered.

"Hana," he said.

I tucked in on myself, trying to disappear. I didn't want him here, not in my space, my life—except I did want to see him. I just didn't want him to see me. Not like this, because I wasn't close to being at my best. Worse still, I'd been pining for him, the one who'd created the grief in my life.

This, this wasn't—no! He couldn't be here with those soulful eyes and that earnest, even worried expression on his face.

I focused my attention on the keyboard, mouse, and stapler resting on its laminated surface.

"Hana, please. I know I shouldn't have come to your work, but I desperately need to talk—"

I didn't even realize I'd picked up the stapler until I released it from my hand. I gaped, shocked, sickened, as it flew through the air, straight toward Paxton Naese's beautiful, rugged face.

Pax must have been off his game, because while he raised his arm, the plastic edge still caught his cheek, flaying the skin open. The offending office supply fell to the floor with a clatter, and we both stared at it. It was safer than looking at him.

I was furious, shocked, and my entire body shook. My teeth chattered. "Oh, oh my…" I whispered, my fingers coming to my lips. "I'm sorry. I'm *so sorry*. That was *wrong* of me. I didn't think, didn't mean…" *But didn't I?*

He gave a nervous chuckle. "Still got that good softball arm, and your aim's spot-on."

I straightened my shoulders and set my chin. "No. I don't. I gave that up years ago." Along with most other physical activity because my leg can't handle it. I was lucky they'd been able to save the mangled mess.

This is me now: an automaton who inputs data for a program she doesn't care about for a life she doesn't want.

As much as I wanted to squeeze my eyes shut, instead I rose from the chair. "Again, I'm so very, very sorry. That was completely uncalled for. I'll clean and bandage your cut."

I stooped to pick up the stapler, but Paxton mirrored me, dropping to his haunches. He looked so handsome, even with the small gash on his high, stark cheekbone. His features had lost the last haze of youth and stood prominent and sharp. His eyes were wary and full of yearning…

And that made me angry. Really angry. He didn't get to yearn. He'd broken up with me. He'd nearly cost me my ability to walk, had definitely cost me the child I would—did—love with all my heart and soul.

Damn him.

Just…damn Paxton Naese. I hated him—*almost as much as I loved the unfeeling, selfish ass.*

No! Gah, where had that thought come from? I didn't love him. I couldn't. That would be ridiculous, especially after everything that had happened because of him.

"You know what? No. I don't owe you anything. Go away, Paxton."

"Hana." He whispered it like a plea.

"What's going on?" Jeremy asked. His shadow fell over us, and I clutched the stapler to my chest as I rose and burrowed under his arm, which he tightened around me. He was thoughtful, kind; he didn't break my heart and ruin me to my very soul.

"Paxton's leaving," I said.

"Hana…" So much emotion in just my name. Paxton's shoulders heaved, his chin dropping. "We *really* need to talk."

"No, we don't. The time for talking was *years* ago."

"Please, don't get stubborn." His eyes darted toward Jeremy.

"Whatever you have to say to me, you can say in front of Jeremy," I told him, insinuating that we were more together than we were. Jeremy enjoyed that immensely, and he kissed my temple and nuzzled into my hair…and I still felt nothing. Only when I stared at Paxton did I feel, and it was a wall of anger so thick, boiling, I wasn't sure I'd ever overcome it.

Because what he was feeling now, with misery shining through his eyes, is what I'd had to suffer for months after the accident, after I'd lost everything I'd wanted.

Paxton's expression shifted from sadness and jealousy to a neutral mask. "All right. I guess, well, I guess I needed closure."

"Why?" I sniped. "You're the one who broke up with me."

Paxton's lips curled into the tiniest smile. "Not because I wanted to." He hesitated but then blew out a breath. "Your mom—"

A growl ripped out of my throat. "Are you *really* going to say my *dead* mother made you break up with me?"

Memories swirled. My mother had never considered Paxton enough for me. I was too brilliant to waste my life with an athlete. I was too delicate to accommodate such a brute. More and more comments, more and more thoughts swirled inside my head.

She'd tried everything to break us up. I knew that. Just as I knew she'd been delighted when Paxton and I had split.

"She's dead? I… *Damn*, Han, I didn't know." Paxton's

shoulders bunched. When he bit his lip, my heart ached for him. I hated to see him nervous.

Why did he seem surprised? Our crash had made the news, mostly because Aiki's driving under the influence had required a trial that caused him to plead for a manslaughter charge. He was still in jail—all of that thanks to me having called my mother and hoped for…something more than her usual dismissal of my feelings. She'd finally proved to be the mother I wanted, and her decision to be there for me had gotten her killed. I straightened my spine and lifted my chin, ignoring Jeremy, who was irritating me with his cuddling.

"What are you trying to say, Pax?" I hadn't wanted my voice to soften, hadn't wanted to use my nickname for him, but his confusion and sadness had gotten to me.

The jerk had always made me feel—and more than I wanted to.

Paxton lifted his eyes and met my gaze. Yearning and anger swirled in their depths. He gestured toward me, seeming almost helpless…lost. "I didn't know."

CHAPTER 3

Paxton

The computer beeped, startling us from the tense grip of our shared past. Hana shrugged out from under the skinny-shit boyfriend's arm and turned with a faint stumble toward the machine, but not before I noted her twisted mouth and the jut of her pixie chin.

She was upset, but with me or her mother?

"It doesn't matter now. That was years ago," she said over her shoulder. "And my mother's no longer able to defend herself."

"I'm sorry," I murmured.

Hana snorted. "Your condolences are *years* too late."

I fisted my hands, my anger with my parents blooming hot. "I didn't know," I said again.

She glanced back at me, frowning. "How is that possible?"

"*I don't know.* I…I thought you sent me a message, telling me you never wanted to see me again."

"I see…" Hana blinked up at me, but the distance between us had grown, and not just with the physical floor space. The skinny shit moved closer to Hana, his hand on the back of her neck, his glare toward me hotter than the sun.

I wanted to rip his hands from her. He shouldn't be touching Hana. *She is mine.*

But she wasn't, and it was my fault. We all knew it, which is why the skinny shit smirked.

"I think you said what you needed to, so why don't you leave, like she asked?"

Much as I didn't want to leave her, especially with him, I needed to regroup—to find out what else I'd missed in Hana's life over the past three years. I looked over his shoulder, wanting to connect with her just for another second, but the skinny shit stepped closer.

"She's mine now," he said, his voice smug. "Whatever was between you is *long* dead and buried. Leave it there."

His words got to me more than I wanted to admit. Because Hana did seem to belong in that lab. And now that I'd seen him, I had to agree that the skinny shit was just the type of man she should have gone for—smart, suave, well-dressed, and solicitous.

I enjoyed astrophysics nearly as much as Hana did, but I wasn't built for the kind of work she loved. I resented having to sit still for too long. Sure, I could code and even create proto-types—I'd chosen to study in a field similar to Hana's before I left college—but honestly, I preferred the physicality of hockey.

Even now, thanks to the emotions flowing through me, I fidgeted. The need to run, hit, skate was strong. So strong.

I willed Hana to meet my eyes again, to see everything in my expression that I didn't want to say, to give me the second chance I hadn't been able to carve out with her because I'd arrived at her house too late that next morning three years ago. I gritted my teeth. Twenty-year-old me was a fucking moron, and twenty-four-year-old me was suffering the consequences.

The skinny shit leaned toward Hana and whispered something in her ear. She stiffened but didn't look up again. "Go away,

Paxton," she murmured. "Please."

The skinny shit smirked as I turned on my heel and left the lab. As I walked down the hall, I heard him coaxing her, followed by Hana's clipped response. *That* actually brought pep to my step. She might be with the guy, but Hana wasn't content.

I used to make her happy. Deliriously so. Just as she had made me.

I could do that again, given the chance. Being a professional athlete, I was known for my stubbornness, and I wasn't ready to give up. Not after one meeting. *Nope.* I'd just have to up my game. Try harder. Do better. Like I did on the ice.

Except... Except Hana was more important than my hockey career, which could end maybe next game or, if I was lucky, in fifteen-years' time. Either way, I wouldn't be able to play in the NHL after some point, but I could still have Hana.

Maybe. Possibly. If I didn't fuck this up worse—or again.

I pulled out my phone and dialed Cruz, who was waiting in the car at the edge of the small green space that I supposed was a lawn. "So?" he asked, picking up on the first ring.

Cruz, for all his size and sheer brutality as a defenseman on the ice, was the biggest marshmallow of us all. Dude watched those Hallmark movies and *told the rest of us* about them. He loved happy endings and was a sad sap whenever there was a puppy or a baby in a commercial. No one laughed or ribbed him for any of this.

We couldn't. He was too invested, too sincere. Too good of a guy. If anyone deserved a happy ending, it was him. So it shocked me that Cruz was single.

"So, Hana was with her skinny-shit boyfriend…" I touched my cheek. "She threw a stapler at me."

"Aggressive," Cruz rumbled with approval. Not that he condoned violence off the ice. He didn't, but he also had three sisters and a widowed mother. Cruz appreciated women who could take care of themselves.

"Not typically." I sighed. "Clearly she wasn't expecting to see me."

"And you brought out heightened emotions?"

"Yeah, but that doesn't mean I'll be able to win her back."

I could see Cruz now. He had his car window down, the late-afternoon air bathing his thickly muscled arm as it rested on the door frame. He shrugged, and I clicked off my phone and shoved it in my pocket. He saw me and did the same, then started the engine.

"Doesn't mean you can't either," he said, continuing our conversation in person as he pulled up.

I settled into the seat, slammed the door, and deflated as I touched my cheek. The pep talk I'd given myself moments before was lost under the weight of seeing the skinny shit's arm around Hana. "Maybe I should have left her alone."

"And spiral down into a useless sack of misery? Nah, man. But you do need to get to the bottom of the situation."

I slumped, not wanting him to say the next words, but this was Cruz, and he was relentless. "You need to call your parents and find out what your mom knows about the situation, what your parents did. Then you need to find out what your parents told Hana and what *she* believes happened. I'm positive there's more to this story than either of you understands." He shot me a look. "More than your folks have told you even now. But you probably loosened their lips by threatening to disown them."

"I didn't threaten to disown them," I said, affronted. "I simply told my father we no longer had a relationship."

Cruz's lips curled in the beginnings of a grin...I thought. His beard was so bushy it was hard to tell. Dude needed a barber to whack that thing back.

I turned in my seat to face him. "Why do you care? I mean, I get that me being content means my head's in the game, but you seem to care a lot about the whole team's happiness."

"Course I care," Cruz snapped, shooting me a surly look. "Why wouldn't I?"

I scratched my head. "Dunno. I mean, it just seems like you're spending time helping us be happy when you could be working on your own life."

Cruz's hands tightened on the steering wheel to the point that it creaked under the pressure. I worried it would snap and we'd career into a building. Instead, Cruz took a long breath in through his nose and let it out slowly. "Yeah, I guess I never told y'all that story. Because it sucks." He shot me a beady eye. "My girl's gone. Basically dead and buried. There's no happiness in the cards for me, man. Not now, not ever. So the best I can do is see your shining happy faces and know I had a part in making it so."

Dead? I gaped. Then I swallowed, but my throat was dry, and I coughed. Once I finished wheezing, I said, "Cruz, that's... *Fuck,* man. I'm sorry."

He stared out the windshield, his shoulders rounded forward. "Me, too. Me, too."

~

"The first task is to show up when the skinny shit isn't there," Cruz said as we holed up in our hotel room for the night. I'd splurged, getting us a nice two-bedroom suite just a couple of miles from Hana's lab. I figured Cruz deserved to sleep in comfort and work out in a state-of-the-art gym after he'd managed to find out where Hana was.

"I'll go over to her place in the morning," I said.

"What happens if the boyfriend's there?" Cruz asked. He dipped his spoon into a weird mashup of cottage cheese and berries, drizzled over the top with honey. Looked like ass to me, but he seemed to enjoy it. Plus, it met the team's nutrition standards.

"I'll beat him up and kidnap her," I joked, though it wasn't really a joke.

Cruz chewed. "Might come to that," he said. "But first, send her a text and let her know you'll be around tomorrow morning and would like to take her to breakfast."

"I don't have her number." I crossed my arms over my chest, glaring at Cruz as if to dare him to make fun of me.

Instead, he shot me a sly smile and pulled a piece of paper from his front pocket. He dropped it in my lap and settled backward, much like a king surveying his lands.

I gaped. "How..."

He waved his hand. "Elementary sleuthing, dear Watson."

I rolled my eyes at his terrible British accent, but I unfolded the paper and tapped the digits into my phone, happy to have

Hana's number again. Once finished, I set my phone down and raised my eyebrows at him. "I didn't think you condoned violence off the ice."

"I don't, normally, but I don't like the skinny shit, as you call him."

"You haven't even met him."

He shook his head. "Don't need to. Know the type. Assholes who think their big brains somehow should push ours around—because we must have littler minds simply because we play sports."

"Well, my guess is that he has more formal education than we do, and from a top-tier university," I countered.

"So? You're smart, Naese. *Real* smart. That's why NASA asked you to come out—you can synthesize all their science-y words and make it so us dumb-jock meatheads can understand."

I laughed and half-heartedly punched his shoulder. "You're just as smart as me. You're the one reading about string theory."

"That blows my mind." He made an explosion sound as he pulled his fingers from the side of his head and heaped another bite of his nasty cottage cheese into his mouth, chewing with obvious relish.

I stared down at my phone, waiting for a response from Hana. None came.

Not then, and not in the hours I sat up, waiting, hoping... Not until I was pulled from a fitful sleep at seven the next morning to the ding of a message.

Hana: Okay.

That's all she wrote back.

Talk about keeping her thoughts and reasons close.

But I rose, showered, shaved, and dressed before I called for a rideshare to take me to the restaurant where she'd said she'd meet me at eight.

When I arrived, I realized the café she'd chosen was just a couple of blocks from her office, and it seemed popular with young professionals. I was ten minutes early, so I sat on the bench out front and texted my mom. It was nearly eleven in New Hampshire, so I knew she was well into her day.

Me: Why didn't you ever tell me Mrs. Sato died? What else happened to Hana's family?

Mom: Oh! You found out.

Me: Yeah, I did. What else have you kept from me?

My mother called me, and I declined it. After a long moment, the bubbles reappeared in our text thread.

Mom: Your dad thought it best we left the Satos alone.

Me: And you just went along with that? Knowing Hana had lost her mother? After the years of her hanging out with us multiple times a week? Do you see how cruel you were to her? How selfish?

I felt myself getting angry all over again. I leaned my head back and shut my eyes, trying to find some level of calm.

Mom: Your father has his reasons, Paxton.

"Well, they're rotten ones," I grumbled.

I checked the time, only to re-check it again seemingly an hour later to find that less than a minute had passed. *Damn*, I was really anxious. Way more than I'd been for any hockey game, even my first professional one.

She'd show. That was one thing about Hana; she followed through. And she'd picked the place and time, so I knew she knew where it was. I shouldn't have arrived so early, because now that I'd given my name to the hostess and let her know I was waiting for the other half of my party, I had nothing to do but pace out front and check my phone.

"Pax?"

I whirled at the sound of Hana's voice. I shaded my eyes and stared into her dark ones.

"Hey," I said with a smile that grew and grew until my cheeks ached. I'd missed her so damn much. Only now that I saw her again did the heaviness I hadn't realized I was carrying ease.

She returned my smile tentatively and touched her fingertips to my small cut. "I'm sorry about this."

"Not a thing," I said.

She bit her lip and shook her head. "It was, too. Don't let me off the hook like that. I behaved badly. Terribly, in fact. I'm sorry, Pax."

"Not as sorry as I am. I deserve way more than a thrown stapler. You have to believe me, Hana. I had no idea about your mother."

She studied me for a long time. Long enough that I felt people shifting closer, whispering, possibly recognizing me. They didn't matter, though. Hana did. I kept my attention locked on her as I waited for her to finish her examination of me. "She died in a car accident. Aiki and I were also in the car."

I sucked in a breath, my muscles tense. If her mother died, the accident must have been bad. "You're okay?" I rasped.

The faintest smile graced her lips. "I didn't die, and I can still get around, so yeah. The doctors said I was lucky."

I clasped her hand between mine. "I really can't imagine what that was like. But I'd like you to tell me. I want to understand."

"Is that Paxton Naese?" a guy in the growing crowd asked. "What's he doing here? Don't they play the Sharks tonight?"

While this part of California wasn't known for hockey, I was on a championship-winning team and one of the faces of the franchise. Clearly, even here, people recognized me.

But I didn't want anything to ruin this moment with Hana; it was too important. I shifted so my back was to the guy who'd asked about me. "Can we go inside?" I asked.

"Yeah—"

"You're Naese, aren't you? The starting winger for the Wildcatters." A small, excited blond sidled up closer, batting her lashes. "Will you give me your autograph?"

The way she said it was suggestive, and Hana's eyebrows rose. I offered her a look that I hoped showed my discomfort and an apology. "Sure, but then I'm having breakfast with my friend."

"You could join us instead," she said, smiling enough to reveal dimples.

I shook my head. "Thanks for the offer, but we'd really like some privacy to catch up." I fished out a pen and signed the receipt she handed me.

"Picture?" she asked, hopeful.

I sighed but nodded, bending my knees and offering a tight smile as she brought up her phone. As soon as it snapped, I snagged Hana's hand and tugged her inside the café. I breathed a sigh of relief to be away from the prying eyes.

"Do you have a table that's out of the way, please?" I asked the hostess. I handed her a fifty.

"Sure." She was a perky college-aged woman with dark hair and eyes. She smiled at us as she grabbed menus. She led us toward a table in the back corner, closest to the kitchen. "It can get a little loud over here," she said, "but no one can see you from the front."

"Perfect." I sighed with satisfaction.

"No problem, Mr. Naese. Good luck with your game tonight."

I offered a weak smile. Once Hana slid into her side of the booth, I slid in on the other, pressing myself as close to the wall as possible.

"Is it always like that when you go out now?" Hana asked.

I didn't want to answer that question honestly, but I knew I must. Hana and I were on rocky ground underlaid with quicksand. I had no choice but to put everything out there and hope—pray—she appreciated the truth.

"It's worse, typically, because most of the places we go are hockey cities."

"Ah, I see," Hana said. She looked down at the menu in front of her.

"Hana, I need to tell you—"

"That my mother bullied and manipulated you into breaking up with me? When Aiki called me this morning for our monthly chat, I confronted him. He told me he kept you from me the morning after you broke my heart."

I blew out a breath, hating those words, hating her straightforward look—as if she no longer had a heart or I could no longer break it. I didn't love either possibility.

A server stopped at the table. Hana ordered French toast and coffee while I ordered a three egg-white omelet with extra vegetables and a matcha latte.

Hana shook her head. "What surprised me was that Aiki said your father and my mother both wanted us to break up. I didn't know your father disliked me—us—so much. That's…shattering."

"Their opinion doesn't matter," I said fiercely. I hesitated, then picked up her hand where it lay on the tabletop. Her fingers were cool, and I resisted the urge to squeeze them. "He and I haven't had much of a relationship in years, and what we do have is definitely strained. I'm angry with him for pushing me to break up with you." I swallowed the pain that had settled in my chest, burning my throat. "I had no idea about the accident. If I'd known, I would have been there, Hana. I would have given up my contract, I would have quit hockey—whatever—to be with you while you grieved your mother."

She disentangled her fingers from mine and took a deep, slow breath. "I believe you, Pax. I do."

"Thank God." I slumped back in the seat. The server brought our drinks, and I offered a weak smile.

When the server departed, I asked, "Will you tell me about the accident?"

Hana stirred in cream and sugar, keeping her attention focused on her cup. I wasn't sure she would answer me, but then she lifted her head, determination set in her features. "It was before the draft. After those pictures of you and Davis at the bar—you with that woman." Her jaw tensed, relaxed, then tensed again. I tried to imagine how I'd have felt if she'd broken up with me and soon thereafter there were pictures of her with another man.

I would have wanted to pound someone to alleviate my devastation. Hana didn't have the hockey outlet, so she typically turned her emotions inward, against herself.

"I was upset." She wrapped her long, delicate fingers around her mug. "Too upset to stay at school where everyone was asking me questions about us."

I closed my eyes. I hadn't thought about that. It had never crossed my mind that people would hound Hana about me leaving. It should have. I should have been more sensitive. *Dammit.*

"I couldn't leave my dorm without questions, so I called my mother."

Hana had to have been desperate to call her mom. But I'd planned to marry her, and all her friends knew that. I took a deep sip of my drink, needing the liquid to ease the dryness in my mouth.

"Aiki and Mom showed up. I almost didn't get in the car because I knew Aiki was going to gloat—tell me what an asshole you were. But at least at home, I thought I'd be able to get away from the questions if I shut myself in my room." She looked over my head, her expression distant.

"But he didn't say anything about you. Looking back, that was my first clue. I didn't realize he was drunk or high or whatever it was until he ran the first red light. I asked him to pull over, to let Mom and me out. To give me the keys. He…he laughed. Said no way. He was still laughing when he ran the next light—head on into another car."

Hana shuddered. "I have no idea how he survived. None. I was lucky because I was in the backseat. Mom died on impact."

She met my gaze. "So did the people in the other car."

"Hana, holy—I'm sorry. I don't... What you went through...I can't imagine."

She was quiet for a long, tense minute. "So, since you didn't know about the accident, I'm guessing you didn't know I was in the hospital for weeks myself?"

I shook my head. "Why?"

"My leg. It got caught when the car rolled." She frowned. "I think it was seven times."

"Holy crap," I breathed.

She bit her lip in that utterly Hana way. It wasn't shy or even flirty. She did it when she was deep in contemplation. "I almost lost my leg," she said slowly. "But that wasn't the worst part."

Dread settled over me, and my diaphragm spasmed. Something dark hovered above us. Her eyes filled with pain and regret. I hated that look, just as I knew I was going to hate the words that came next.

Still, I wasn't prepared. Nothing could have prepared me for the emotional blow.

"I miscarried during my second surgery," she said.

CHAPTER 4
Hana

I watched emotions flicker over Paxton's face. The one that stuck with me was sadness. Or maybe it was regret.

"You were pregnant?" he whispered.

I nodded.

"And the baby died?" His voice cracked and his lip wobbled.

"Never really had a chance to live," I responded, trying to be pragmatic when all I really wanted was to curl up in a ball, preferably in his lap. The loss hit me hard, a sucker punch, just as it always did. But this time it was both better and much worse because I could share the pain with Pax.

"I was probably seven, maybe as many as nine weeks along."

"And you never called to tell me?" Accusation flashed in his dampening eyes.

"I did."

He clenched his jaw tightly enough that I heard his teeth squeak. "My dad gave me a new phone after Aiki took mine. You wouldn't have had that number."

"Aiki told me that this morning, too," I said.

So many lies and misdirections that had hurt us both. Paxton's complexion had gone ashen. This wasn't the conversation he'd thought he'd be having in this bright, loud diner this morning. The longer I watched him struggle, the more my heart ached for him.

He hadn't known—about my mother, about me, about the baby.

The bitterness that had encased my heart cracked and fell away. I'd never understood how Pax could prove so unfeeling. I'd thought him ruthless toward me in my time of need. Now I realized he was still that sensitive boy I'd fallen for, just in a hulking, stunning body.

"I...don't know what to say." He blinked at me, hurting from a past neither of us could change.

"What is there to say, really?" I inhaled as I stared down at my hands. My nails were short and rounded, buffed to a shine. I'd never been one to fuss over nail polish, though I enjoyed the manicure treat days Paxton's mother used to take me on. Looking back, I think I mostly enjoyed the company of a woman—a mother—who was interested in my thoughts and interests. I cleared my throat, unable to force words past the choking pressure in my throat.

"Hana, going through that *alone*..."

I offered a small smile as I finally breathed past the pain. "Your dad knew. I told him and Hugo."

Hugo was one of my older brothers. Devon, my other brother, owned a brewpub in our hometown. Hugo worked with my father at the university as a conditioning coach.

I watched Paxton's face contort again. Each revelation was a blow. I hated hurting him—always had—but he needed to know the whole of his father's treachery. I'd thought *for sure* Pax would come when I'd called the Naeses' house after not being able to get through to him. I'd had to use the hospital's phone because mine was destroyed in the wreck. Mr. Naese had answered, made appropriately sympathetic comments, and promised to pass the information along to Paxton.

Based on Pax's expression, that had never happened.

How stupid of *me*, really. Paxton had never been anything other than thoughtful, and I was ridiculous for failing to realize that before this moment. I'd been in too much pain, then grieving, then angry, to think through Pax's lack of response. It had just seemed par for the course, the way things were going for me then. But it was all built on lies, omissions, and assumptions.

I was in the sciences. I knew exactly what to do with assumptions: never, ever accept them. I stared down into my coffee and a glimmer of something bright, something beautiful, cut with painful precision right through my chest.

Was it? Could it be…

Hope. Over the ringing in my ears, I heard Paxton speaking. I raised my head and blinked at him, seeing him clearly—really—for the first time since he'd broken up with me. Here he was, his expression shattered, his voice breaking, as he began to cope with the loss we'd experienced—that we should have experienced together.

"Hana. I don't… I don't know how to fix this. I…" Bright red color seeped across Paxton's cheekbones, and he burst out, "My father is an epic dick, and I'm never talking to him again."

My anger from those days came back, choking me. Yes, Mr. Naese was indeed an *epic* dick, and I never wanted to speak to him again either. But that wouldn't hold, because Paxton had been close to his father, and I wouldn't be the reason he lost that connection. More, I was going to have to sit down across from the man who'd worked to cut me out of his son's life and ask him why. That would not be an easy conversation, and I wouldn't like the answers, but I deserved them.

"I broke my new phone the night of the draft," Paxton said.

At my expression, he rushed on to explain. "I wanted to call you, but everyone was telling me not to. I was heartsick that Houston had passed me over, and I'd left you, and…" He closed his eyes and a tiny, self-deprecating smirk flitted across his lips. "I threw that phone out the window of a cab."

"You?" I gasped, shocked to my core. Paxton was levelheaded, cool no matter what came at him.

"I sure did. Then I kicked my dad out of the cab and went drinking with Davis." He grimaced. "That asshole got me wasted. I don't remember much after the first beer."

I picked up my coffee and took a long sip, trying to wipe the bitterness off my tongue. "That would explain the pictures of you partying."

Paxton's eyes closed. "I wasn't dating those women. Though I hooked up with some of them in the ensuing months, hoping it would make me feel better about breaking up with you."

"Did it work?" A morbid curiosity bubbled up, along with the rancid taste of jealousy, choking me.

He opened his eyes, and his gray-green irises seemed to darken. "Not even a little bit."

"I'm sorry to hear that." And I was, though I wasn't.

"Not as sorry as I am. For everything that happened then."
He reached across the table and took my hand. He didn't try to

slide his palm against mine, clearly sensing that was too intimate a gesture. But he cradled the back of my hand in his much larger one, making me feel dainty, small…fragile. "Then the pictures came out, and your friends were harassing you. That's why you called your mother—that night, those pictures." Pax looked sick. "I saw them recently because team PR had all the guys go through everything that's online and attached to us. *Fuck*! I look like such a douche in those."

He did. And not the man I'd thought I'd known. That had left me questioning everything between us and had led, in part, to the spiral I'd found myself trapped in these past few years. I'd thought I'd made progress toward learning to accept and love who and what I was, but being with Paxton now brought about a dizzying array of emotions I didn't know how to process.

"Hana, I'm so, so—"

"No." I set the coffee down with a distinct thump. "No. It's over. We can't change that, and guilt won't make it different."

"But—"

"No, Paxton." I shook my head. I stared at the kitchen doors for a moment. "It won't change what happened," I murmured again. "We're here today. I'm fine."

And I was. Though I wanted to blurt out my depression, my dislike of my career, and my worries about my future. I wanted to treat Paxton as the confidant he'd once been. Instead, I said, "I get that you didn't know this, and it's a shock, but I don't think I can trust you. With me."

The waiter walked toward us, carrying our plates of steaming food. I used that as an excuse to extricate my hand from Paxton's grasp. I settled back into the booth, my heart racing, my thoughts roiling like a soup set too high. I might well overflow, burning those around me before I burned out.

We remained silent, and Paxton picked at his meal, just as I did mine.

Finally he set his fork down. "Are you serious about him? The guy in your lab?"

I swallowed the bite I'd been chewing for much longer than necessary and dabbed at my lips. "Jeremy? We're not dating…"

Paxton focused his intensity on me, and I liked it. I'd always liked him looking at me. "He'd like to be," he said.

"Yes, well, thankfully, he asked for my input on the matter."

Paxton winced.

I sighed. "I'm sorry. That was cruel."

He inhaled as he gripped the edge of the table. "No, it's fair. I made the choice to break up with you—not your mom or my dad or your brother. *I* let the pressure from their concerns outweigh what I knew in my heart: you're it for me, Hana. I met my soulmate when I was seven years old."

His quiet words soothed the ragged pieces of me as I wondered how, if he'd ever loved me as I loved him, he could have left me the way he did. He met my gaze, unflinching, though I felt his heel jiggling up and down through the table's thick metal base and pedestal, where I rested my feet. He might appear calm and collected, but this conversation—my response—mattered to him. *A lot.*

"Would you be willing to get to know me again?" he asked.

"Why, Paxton?" I asked. "Why now? Why ask this of me?"

He went completely still. "Because I've been absolutely miserable without you, Han. I can't keep pretending I don't *need* you with every single breath."

CHAPTER 5
Paxton

I paid for our partially eaten meals soon after my heartfelt statement because Hana had fallen silent once more.

"I need to think about what you said. What you want. What *I* want," she told me as we exited the restaurant. Her limp had become more pronounced. I wanted to ask her about it, but I doubted she wanted to rehash more of our past right now.

We were both raw.

A group of hockey fans who must have been waiting converged on me then, asking for autographs and photos. Hana slipped away—once again taking my heart with her.

I wished I could have expressed how much she meant to me, but I hadn't gotten through to her. Not really. That had to do with my father, his manipulations—his *reasons*, my mother had said—but I didn't have a clue why he was so adamant that we stay apart.

A few minutes later, I caught a glimpse of Hana as she stood at the edge of the parking lot, her head tilted to the side as she watched me interact with the group of ten or so college students. I'd managed to text Cruz, and he'd replied that he'd pick me up. I was thankful when he arrived. I caught Hana's eyes and tipped my head toward the car, asking silently if she wanted a ride. She shook her head, relief sweeping over her features before she ducked her head to hide the expression.

I told my fans goodbye and pulled myself into the rental car, slamming the door shut with a thud.

"How'd it go?" Cruz asked.

"I'm not sure. I may have overplayed my hand," I replied. My stomach was still knotted, and I shook out my arms, struggling with the tension pulsing through my muscles.

Cruz pursed his lips and stared out the window for a moment before he shook his head. "By being honest? Doubt it. That's your girl, right?"

"Yeah. Well, she's not mine. She's not sure she wants to be, and after what she told me today, I get it." *Fuck, did I get it.* "But at least she's not with the skinny shit."

Cruz rumbled. "That's something. Hang on, I'll do you a solid."

Before I could ask what he meant, Cruz hopped from the car and strode toward Hana. He offered her his hand and gestured toward where I sat. She answered, confusion tugging at her straight, black brows. Her skin glowed in the sunlight.

She took my breath away. She always had, and in this moment, I knew she always would.

Cruz pulled out a card and handed it to her. She took it and stared. Then she lifted her head and met my gaze. She held there before she returned her attention to Cruz. Whatever she said made him smile. He gave her a gentle cuff on the shoulder before he headed back to me.

"What did you do?" I asked as he settled back in the driver's seat, panic seeping into my limbs. "If you fucked this up—"

"I invited her to the game and gave her a pass so she could

get into the locker room area afterward. That's what you wanted, right? To have time with her, to have her get to know you and us and see if you two would fit?"

I nodded, though I resented Cruz prodding me. I was handling the situation. Maybe not well or with any suaveness at all, but I had been handling it.

Cruz drove past Hana, where she still stood, clutching the pass in her hand. I waved. She began to raise her hand but let it fall. She whipped her head around, and I noted the skinny shit striding toward her, his mouth twisted with anger. His eyes moved toward me, and I noted the hot, ugly jealousy in them before Cruz pulled out onto the road.

"My mother has a saying," Cruz said. "Only the most stubborn survive. That's been true for me in hockey. You think many kids from the wrong neighborhood in a city that doesn't have a professional team end up in the NHL?"

"I know the statistics, man. That's why I do the outreach to the Fifth Ward." That was one of the roughest neighborhoods in Houston—ironically, perched near the downtown area where hundreds of millions of dollars flowed through the city with lightning speed.

Yes, kids like Cruz, who'd been raised on the edge of the Fifth Ward, were lucky if they had schoolbooks in their classrooms. No lie. The Wildcatters had bought the elementary school new textbooks, and I'd watched six kids—mostly boys—cry as they touched them for the first time.

Poverty *sucked*.

"It's not just the ability to get on ice," Cruz said. "It's the cost of the equipment and teams, travel—all of it is too much for many families. Definitely for mine. So I figured it out. I wasn't going to let my sisters go hungry because I might have a chance at the pros."

"How'd you do it?" I asked. Cruz seemed like an open book, but I actually knew very little about his formative years.

He glanced over, and I would've sworn his lips curled up in a self-satisfied smile. "Sometimes, you need to beg."

CHAPTER 6

Hana

"Why did you meet him?" Jeremy asked, his voice a curious mix of whine and imperiousness that grated on my already-scraped-raw nerves. I shoved my hands in my pockets outside the restaurant, stowing the pass Lennon Cruz had handed me even as I tracked their car. I wasn't sure how I felt about the pass, what I wanted to do, and Jeremy's presence wasn't making that any better.

"*Why*, Hana? He's old news," Jeremy stated. "Your clichéd high-school phase. Why do women think athletes are hot? They're sweaty and stupid—useless to society." He perked up and refocused on me. "You have to admit, with everything you're working on here, your life is way better."

"Do I?" I asked.

Jeremy grabbed my arm, pulling me out of my foggy haze. Aiki used to grab me. My mother, too. Grab me, shake me, put me where they wanted me because they could—because I allowed it and because they wanted to show who was in charge in my life. *Not me.* That was the clear answer from my mother, from Aiki, and now, from Jeremy. My thoughts, my feelings were secondary. So much for the solicitude he'd shown before. Now, because of a little potential competition, Jeremy's true self had burst forth.

No wonder I hadn't wanted him; I must have sensed this ugliness lurking below the urbane surface. My biology professor had once told the class we all could feel danger, but we'd learned to suppress that gut instinct.

"Hey! Are you coming?" called Esther, one of my colleagues and another of Jeremy's employees. She came toward us, shoving her glasses up her nose as her eyes moved from Jeremy's tight grip to my face and the tension between us. She gave me a questioning look. Whatever expression she received back—my face was stiff with anxiety—appeared to have an effect.

"Let's go, Jeremy. We need to eat before we get back to the lab to finish these current projections, right? You wanted to go over the lift mechanism, you said."

"I expect you to be there, running that data, when we get to the office, Hana." Jeremy's voice dripped like acid over me.

I didn't *want* to be there. I didn't want to be near him, not if he thought he could bully me into a decision. Yet even with all those emotions choking me, I nodded.

Old habits died hard, I supposed, and as much as I hated to admit it, I was used to deferring. To Jeremy now, it seemed, and for years before that, to my mother's will.

I sighed in relief when Jeremy's fingers uncoiled from my arm. I pulled back with such speed that I stumbled. Esther steadied me with a gentle hand. "He's done this before," she breathed into my ear before herding Jeremy away. "And I'm going to let Lennon know."

What, exactly, had he done before? Who was Lennon? Why would Esther tell me any of this? I wasn't sure what to make of her comments, and my head ached too much to sort through that set of information.

I watched them walk away, and I didn't go to the lab; I called a rideshare to go home.

I didn't have a car, and I hadn't driven much even before the car accident. Once I'd arrived on the West Coast, I hadn't needed a car, for which I'd been so very thankful.

Maybe if I'd pushed back harder, been more rebellious in high school, by forcing the issue to buy myself a car…or insisting on spending more time with Pax, I'd have the life I wanted now. I pulled out the pass Cruz had given me and flipped it over, considering. *What would the life I want look like?*

The first thing to surface was Paxton. He wasn't wrong when he'd said we were soulmates. I'd missed him with every single breath I'd taken these past three years—the way I would miss not being able to walk. I was sure of that comparison because for weeks, I hadn't been able to walk. And for months after that, I'd struggled to get my leg strong enough to hold my weight. Such a simple thing, walking—until you couldn't.

I didn't *want* to depend on Paxton for my happiness. He'd already proven once that I shouldn't. He'd left me, and I'd been miserable. Only a fool would believe he'd changed, that he wouldn't hurt me again, right?

I was a fool.

These thoughts percolated through my mind as I walked into my efficiency apartment, curled up in my blanket, and replayed the morning's conversation with Paxton over and over. He'd made me feel good. Respected. Safe. Loved.

Happiness—that emotion I'd missed but could barely imagine—drifted upward, its sweetness like a tempting flower.

But if I took what Paxton seemed to be offering, would I have to leave the project? Lose myself in him as my mother had always worried I would?

I didn't know. And because I didn't, I stayed huddled in my bed.

I woke, groggy from dark dreams, to my ringing phone. This was why I rarely napped. I never woke properly from a mid-day sleep. "What?"

Not my normal answer, but I was still out of it. What had I dreamed? Something to do with Paxton being hurt—and Jeremy had been there.

"Hana, you need to get over here now," Esther nearly shrieked into the phone. "There's something wrong with the simulations."

"No, there isn't. I triple-checked them." I was sure my math was right. Unless someone—*Jeremy*—had changed the projections, there was no way the simulation wouldn't run smoothly.

"Jeremy's going ballistic."

I yawned. "Not sure why that's my problem."

"He's talking about removing you from the project," Esther said. "Hana, he may fire you."

"Oh." Well, *that* would be a major problem, but I couldn't imagine Jeremy following through on his threat. I was the only person who really understood the physics of the structure. As Jeremy had pointed out many times: I was integral to his team.

I looked over at the clock, trying to orient myself. "I'm going to be late," I exclaimed.

"You already are," Esther said.

"Not to the lab. To Pax's game."

"Listen to me," she sputtered. "Jeremy's dead serious about firing you. And angry."

I absorbed that information. "He *hurt* me this morning."

Esther grunted. "I'm not surprised, honestly. He's obsessed with you."

"We'll have to talk more later, Esther. Good luck with Jeremy. And for the record, I triple-checked that data. The only way the simulation failed is if someone wanted it to."

CHAPTER 7

Paxton

I pondered Cruz's comment about stubbornness and hockey as I strapped on my skates later that afternoon. The rest of the team had arrived, and we were headed out on the ice in San Jose's arena for a short practice before our game. I was looking forward to getting out there, hoping the physicality, even if it was light and against my friends, would help reduce the gnawing aggression I felt every time I thought about Hana with that garbage of a skinny-shit excuse for a man.

He was going to pull something with her. I knew it. I hoped *she* knew it.

"Let's get out there and see how the ice flows," Coach Whittaker told us.

Maxim, Stolly, and Cormac bounced up off the bench like excited puppies. They all wore shit-eating grins. That's what a good woman did for a man. I was happy for them, even as jealousy left a terrible, metallic taste in my mouth.

Hana had been jealous earlier, even as she'd asked me about my hookups. I didn't want to discuss those with her, ever, but she had a right to know about my years without her. Just as I was going to have to learn about her time without me. Well, if I could talk her into giving me a second chance.

I didn't deserve it, but that wasn't going to stop me. I might well beg, like Cruz had suggested. Because when something was that important, you did whatever you needed to do to secure it. Though if Hana's past was filled with more of the skinny shit or other guys, I was going to detest every single second of her recounting.

"I thought you came out here to lose the scowl," Stol said as he skated past.

Bastard was living his dream. He'd married his fling and had a kid. I realized with a start that if Hana had had our child, he or she would be a couple of years older than Stolly's little girl. I'd have the oldest kid on the team.

"Leave him be," Cruz grumbled as he edged Stol with his shoulder. "He's processing."

"Ah," Maxim said, nodding. "She didn't drop to her knees and say you were a god and admit she'd been pining for you?"

"Who the fuck would do that?" Cormac wanted to know. "The garbage that comes out of your mouth."

"What?" Maxim said. "That would be romantic."

"That would be *mortifying*," Stol said, eyes wide. "I love Millie's fire."

Maxim burst out laughing as he skated ahead.

"Dude likes to mess with us," Cormac noted. "Don't worry. I'll think of something to get even with his stupidity."

"On it," Cruz said. "I already filched his apple butter. It's a *tub* of the stuff. We'll eat it in front of him before the game. That'll get him all riled up."

Cormac rubbed his hands together, grinning broadly. "I love this plan."

"San Jose won't," I said.

"That's why it's a good one," Cruz noted.

We continued to skate, warming up our legs, but my mind drifted back to Hana. I didn't think the skinny shit would hurt her, but I hadn't liked the way he talked to her. I needed to make sure she was safe.

Cruz appeared next to me, matching my stride. "She's fine," he said. "The dude, Jeremy, the one you call skinny shit, is her boss."

"How do you know that?"

Cruz smirked. "Insider knowledge."

"You're hiding something," I decided. "Not just about Hana, but in *your* life. Come on, what is it?"

Cruz shrugged. "Not a thing to worry about."

I snorted. Like I believed him.

We collected our hockey sticks and began drills, my mind eased by Cruz's comments but still flooded with Hana's expression. I sighed as I missed a pass from Stolly, who shouted at me, raising his gloves in frustration.

Coach had his arms crossed over his chest as he glared. "All right. You guys are done for now. Rest up, grab a bite—you know the drill."

As I stepped off the ice to head to the locker room, Coach fell into step beside me. "You need to get your head in the game."

"I know."

"I gave you a lot of leeway, Naese. Don't make me regret it."

"You did. I'll be ready for the game," I assured him. And I was determined to make that true, so I went to eat with Cruz and tried my hardest to chill out.

By the time we returned to get ready for the game, I did feel clearer, more focused, though I couldn't pinpoint why. When we'd arrived at the arena earlier today, I'd asked Sandy, the administrative staffer who had flown in with the team from Houston, to let me know if Hana picked up her ticket at will-call. Once we were seated in the locker room and Coach Whittaker had finished his debrief, Sandy gave me a thumbs-up. *Hana was in her seat.* Now I had butterflies dancing through my belly, making my hands a little shaky as I wrapped my stick. I needed to calm down all over again.

"You okay?" Cormac asked.

"Hana's here."

"Oh. Cool." He smiled. "Where's she sitting? I can have some of the CATS talk to her."

"I don't know if she'd handle that well—"

"Already sorted," Cruz said. "She's with Ida Jane."

"Wish Keelie could have come," Cormac said, suddenly morose. "She would have liked to meet Hana."

"Did Keelie stay at home with Brooks?" I asked.

Cormac perked up. "Yeah, and she said he smiled today. He's sleeping better, too. Six whole hours."

"That's great, man."

A pang hit me as I realized *again* that I could have had a kid. I could be the one bursting with pride because the tot slept several hours in a row. Maybe by now we would even have a second little peanut on the way—if Hana was interested in more kids, of course.

Maxim tossed stuff around in his locker. "Where's my apple butter?" he asked.

"Here," Cruz said.

I whistled as I noted the size. That was a *huge* jar.

"You're sharing this," he informed Maxim. "I don't want to hear a word! You don't want to end up over your weight limit." Cruz pulled out a container of plastic spoons and disposable bowls. "And if I see you trying to hoard this kind of thing again, I'm taking you down."

"Like to see you try," Maxim snapped.

"Leave it, guys," Cormac said, his tone easy. Everyone listened to him. Maxim and Cruz settled down, maybe because Maxim was now snarfing apple butter. Dude was addicted to the stuff.

Stolly's phone rang, and he dove for it, crooning into the receiver. I would have rolled my eyes at how lovesick the sap was if I didn't want the same thing—and just like that, my thoughts returned, again, to Hana.

"Put that liquid candy down, Maxim. Now. Get your heads out of your butts and into the game," Coach said as he strolled into the room. How he knew Cormac was staring daggers at Cruz before he even entered was pure magic.

"Off that phone, Stol," Coach said. He finally looked up from his clipboard. "Paloma's on standby if Millie needs anything. Now, I want to go over the plan of attack one more time before we warm up."

The game was a bruiser, but I relished the aggressive play because it required my full focus. No time to worry about how I'd left the situation with Hana or get my hopes up about a future she hadn't admitted to wanting.

I slammed a defenseman into the boards with my shoulder

and turned to block his stick as he tried to reach for the puck. I slapped around his flailing and shot the puck up toward Stol, who gave his wrist a gentle flip and slipped the puck into the net between the goalie's outstretched arm and leg.

The blue light swirled, and the crowd grew quieter, except for the cheering from our CATS section behind the bench. Cormac patted my helmet and Cruz whacked my shoulder while the rest of the team congratulated Stol.

Yeah, the two of us made a great offensive duo, but without Cormac, Cruz, and Maxim blocking San Jose's offense, we wouldn't have had so much puck time. This group of men worked together as a seamless unit, one we'd been trying to build in our second and third lines. I was beginning to realize that our closeness off the ice helped us play better together in the rink—no doubt another reason Coach was keen on us getting together often.

San Jose came roaring out in the next period, seeming determined to tie the game. The ferociousness heated up, and I took an elbow to the same cheek Hana had hit with the stapler. The team medic pulled me off the ice to have the gash cleaned and bandaged. I glanced over while the trainer worked on me, catching a glimpse of Hana, who sat in the seat next to Ida Jane. She wore a simple blue sweater and dark leggings tucked into calf-high boots. Her hair was pulled back from her face and in a long, thick braid that had settled over one shoulder. A few wisps of Hana's blue-black hair framed her face. Her brown eyes were large with worry. When I offered her a wave, she sent back a tight smile.

Ida Jane leaned closer to Hana and spoke into her ear. Hana

nodded but kept her gaze on me, not bothering to look when the crowd gasped then booed.

I wasn't surprised that Ida Jane had introduced herself nor that she'd taken Hana under her wing. These games were a lot more to handle than the high school versions.

When I looked back at the ice, Maxim had an offensive player against the boards, and Cormac was trying to sweep the puck from between the guy's skates. A collective groan went up as Cormac scraped the puck clean and shot it forward to Stolly. He laid into the slap shot, but the goalie blocked it with his padded shin.

I returned my attention to Hana and found her staring at me. I winked, which led to another smile.

"Stop that," the medic said. "Now that the cut's clean, I'll get the glue in there before I put on the bandage."

"Sorry, Derry. Just letting my girl know I'm okay."

"After you're treated," Derry said, never taking his eyes from my cheek. "Done." He pulled off his gloves and gave me a nod.

I headed toward Coach. "I'm good," I said.

Coach nodded, his arms crossed, eyes never leaving the play on the ice. "Take a breather. The rookie's got something to prove, and we're going to see if he can manage to do so."

I grumbled, frustrated with the idea of a twenty-one year old coming for my spot. Not that I was *that* much older, but I had two and a half seasons with the NHL under my belt, and Stol and I were practically unstoppable when we paired up.

"Hana saw you play," Coach said, seeming to read my mind— and the thoughts I hadn't been *willing* to think. "She's duly impressed. Now, let me win this game so I don't have to deal with the media vultures picking at my bones later."

"Yes, Coach."

The puck slid toward our new goalie, Hansen, who'd taken over from Adam Kramer when he retired at the end of last season. Thankfully, both the coaching staff and Adam had wanted him to continue to be part of the team. So Adam now handled training and nutrition for our goalies, Hansen and Pedersen.

Coach looked over at me as the guys all took a quick breather. "I like her," he said, tipping his head up toward Hana.

"How do you know?" I asked.

"We chatted while you were warming up. Smart woman. Brilliant, in fact."

"She is."

"Does she keep up with you on all that aerospace stuff?"

I smiled. "She's where I learned it."

Coach chuckled, nodded, and returned his focus to the game. "Sit. Rest. Hydrate. You're back in three if I don't see the rook producing."

I put in another fifteen minutes on the ice during the third period, and it was rougher than the first. My ribs ached from the multitude of elbows I'd taken, but I'd managed another assist, this time to the rookie, who Coach had kept on the line, pulling Bonnie, our old-timer.

Bonnier, who we called Bonnie, was thirty-six and showing his age. He didn't have the speed Stol or I did, but he was crafty, with a depth of knowledge about the game we hadn't yet achieved. Still, it was becoming clear that Bonnie was going to have to hang up his skates, and soon. I hated the idea, just as I'd hated Adam choosing to retire. Change wasn't really my thing.

I looked up at Hana after we'd shaken hands with the other team at the end. She was staring at me, so I mouthed, "*Come down.*"

She'd know I meant the locker room, as I'd had Ida Jane pass along the invitation to meet me there earlier. Now it was time to see whether Hana was open to more than the closure we'd begun to get this morning. If she came, I'd find out if she was interested in pursuing something new, better with me.

Hana bit her plump, pink lip, clearly hesitant. She leaned over toward Ida Jane and said something. Ida Jane nodded, and the two of them rose from their seats. The guys corralled me down the tunnel, and I didn't see where the women went.

Two TV crews waited to talk to me about the game, and I did my best to show them the respect their viewers deserved, but all I wanted was to get into the shower and see if Hana was waiting. If so, I'd take her out for a late dinner, or maybe invite her back to my hotel room—no, bad idea. She'd think I wanted sex.

Which I did, because *sex*, but now wasn't the time for that. We needed to heal the breach I'd created between us and find a way to move forward with our relationship, whatever that would be.

CHAPTER 8
Hana

I inhaled a long, deep breath of the ice-tinted air as I looked around the arena. Fans were headed toward the exits while the shiny Zamboni made its first lazy circuit across the ice.

"This was *very* different than his high school games," I whispered.

"It gets easier," said Ida Jane, a petite woman with honey-colored hair and a bright smile, likely noting my growing discomfort. She'd introduced herself to me at the beginning of the game, putting me at ease as she told me stories about her husband, Maxim, and Naese, between cheering on the Wildcatters. She was fun and easy to talk to, and I was glad she'd said something because I'd been slipping into my head.

She stretched as we continued up the aisle to the concourse. "Come on. We'll head down to the locker room. Silas—the guys call him Coach because he's the head coach—usually lets us into his office. He travels with some high-quality cocoa. His daughter, Trixie, loves the stuff."

"So we're just going to take over his office while the guys get cleaned up and sip the coach's hot chocolate?"

"Pretty much. Once the guys finish showering and interviews, they'll come find us there."

"But…" No, I didn't have more to add to that statement.

After a beat, Ida Jane offered a shrug. "It's a bit boring, but that's the truth of being a professional athlete spouse." She led me up the stairs and then down an internal flight. She flashed a badge at a security guard, who stood in front of some double doors.

"Do you have your pass?" Ida Jane asked.

"Oh!" I fumbled in my pocket, pulling out the paper Cruz had given me earlier. The security guard read it and opened the door, speaking into his walkie talkie. We headed down a noisier corridor, filled with reporters and players. The players were sweat soaked, some still holding their gear.

I gawked at the scene as Ida Jane led me toward a door at the end of the hall. She knocked, and Coach Whittaker told us to enter.

"Ah, good! You're here," he said. "There's the hot water and some mugs. I need to run into the presser in a couple of minutes." He offered me a broad smile. "I know Paxton's going to be glad to see you."

Silas Whittaker was big, like the players, and I assumed he'd played before he began coaching. He towered over Ida Jane and me, just as Paxton did. There was something…warming about his size.

"He had a good game tonight," Coach Whittaker added. "Clearly you being here brought out the fire that's been missing all season."

"Thanks," I said, dazed. Had I entered an alternate reality? I felt off-kilter, as if these people knew much more of my story than I did theirs.

I guessed that was because, as Ida Jane had said, Paxton had talked about me. I wasn't sure how to feel about that. He'd never reached out, hadn't shown any interest in years. Now, suddenly, he wanted me in his life again. I'd had whiplash from the accident, and this sensation was similar—just as disconcerting.

Ida Jane got to work preparing cocoa as Coach Whittaker peered at me kindly. I felt like a deer caught in headlights. I wanted to say something. Licking my lips, I opened my mouth.

"They're ready for you, Coach," a young woman in a Wildcatters polo announced.

He nodded, then began patting his pockets. He reminded me of my dad, looking for his glasses. A pang of loss hit hard and fast. My father had been my world, but he'd died when I was young—right before we moved from Brooklyn to the small community in Connecticut where I'd met Paxton.

I wondered if we would have moved had my father survived his aneurism. I also wondered if staying in Brooklyn would have saved me a world of pain.

But we hadn't; my mother had been determined to move even before my father's death, and we'd been ensconced in a new house two short months after his funeral.

I still missed my dad. My mother...not so much.

"Your glasses are atop your head," I offered.

"Ah! Thanks. Yes, well, I better go deal with the press. Let's chat again soon, Hana."

He smiled again before he strolled out. I turned my attention to Ida Jane. "You realize it's like I walked into Wonderland, right?"

"Because we know more about you than you do us? Or because we're all rooting for Naese and you to find a happy ending?" She sipped from a mug, smacked her lips, and practically purred. "It's delicious!"

She picked up the other mug and handed it to me. "I…I guess." I stared down into the dark liquid as I gathered my courage and met Ida Jane's clear blue eyes. "Paxton and I haven't seen each other in years. He broke my heart." I shook my head. "He never came to see me in the hospital." My voice broke, but I blinked back the threatening tears.

Ida Jane raised an eyebrow. "I can tell you with absolute certainty that he didn't know," she said softly. She took another sip of her drink and met my gaze over the top. "I can also tell you there's something strange about how Naese's parents kept your hospitalization from him."

I stared back down into the cocoa, frozen for a moment. Yes, I believed so, too.

"Naese told Cruz, who told Cormac, Maxim, and Stolly, that he'd cut his parents out of his life. For good."

I sipped the sweet, rich brew. "I know how important Naese's family is to him—"

"And he'd put you *before* them now that he knows what they did, what they hid," Ida Jane said. She shook her head and raised her free hand. "I'm sorry. I'm totally overstepping my place. I just want to see Naese happy. He deserves it." She smiled. "And now that I've met you, I want you two to be together and as crazy-happy as Maxim and I are." Her smile softened. "I can *feel* how right you are for each other, and I know he loves you so very much."

"*He loves you so very much.*" The words echoed in my head.

Hadn't I told myself that when we went to different universities? When I saw him less and less thanks to his hockey schedule? Even when he told me we should break up because his schedule would be too hard on me...

But I'd been wrong about Paxton then, and Ida Jane as wrong now. Abandonment wasn't love. Not after the accident, but *before*. Paxton had thrown me away without regard for my feelings and without the respect our relationship deserved, and I couldn't pretend otherwise.

I set the half-filled mug down on the edge of the desk. The constant anger I'd barely learned to leash now swirled upward, choking me. I didn't know Ida Jane, and I couldn't be sure I knew Paxton, could I? He was not the person I'd *thought* he'd been before he left me, and I had only just met the person he was today. "You know what? I can't do this."

Ida Jane kept her expression neutral, almost as if she'd expected my response. "What exactly can't you do?"

"Pretend that I'm fine with the way he broke up with me. With the hookups afterward, with his sudden reappearance. The reporters. This world. All of it."

She nodded, her eyes never leaving mine. "Well, at least you know."

I bit my lip to keep from snapping a response. Ida Jane had been kind to me. I wouldn't repay her with surliness; I wouldn't react like my mother. "Thank you," I said. I headed toward the door, my leg aching with each step, reminding me why I shouldn't even consider the fairy tale I'd never get with Paxton.

I was better off in the quiet of the lab. Unassuming and

unknown. I didn't want this life.

"For the record, he was happier tonight, more focused, than I've ever seen him," Ida Jane called.

My lips twisted. "Don't presume to understand my history," I said stiffly, my hand on the doorknob, my back to her. "He broke *a lot* of promises."

"If you come to another game, I'll tell you how I learned about Maxim's hookup history," Ida Jane said casually, as if we'd remain friendly.

I shook my head. There wouldn't be a next time. "Bye."

Getting back to my apartment took much longer than I'd expected, and I was exhausted by the time I reached my door. I gasped when I flipped on the lights to my studio and found Jeremy lounging on my bed in the far corner. He'd mussed the red silk duvet that I'd inherited from my father's mother, his shoes leaving dirty streaks on the fragile material.

He glared at me, and I glared back.

"What are you doing in here?" I asked.

"Waiting for you," he said.

"How…"

"Your neighbor thinks I'm charming," he said, flashing a dimpled smile.

Celeste had let Jeremy into my place? Oh, we were having words. She had a key for emergencies—like a catastrophic bathroom flood. Not to let in annoying would-be suitors with an ego problem.

I narrowed my eyes and straightened my spine. "You need

to leave. Now."

He rose, his expression set, inflexible. "No, *you* need to *listen*." He stalked closer until he towered over me. "The simulation today didn't pan out. I'm going to have to re-run it. You're off the project."

That was a blow. A big one. A terrible one for my career and my finances. I couldn't really afford more than a month, maybe six weeks if I was very, very careful.

I clenched my jaw and glared back. "If that's the case, then you *definitely* need to get out of my space and my life."

Jeremy stared down at me, waiting. I stared back, my jaw set.

"You're supposed to ask—" He cut himself off. With effort, he wiped his expression and sneered. "Good luck working in aeronautics."

"Don't ever—and I mean *ever*—come to my home again."

Jeremy stormed off, and I collapsed into the chair, staring sightlessly out the window.

Many bridges had burned tonight. In fact, my entire life was in smoldering ruins. But even as I stared outside, a lightness filled my chest, at odds with the whirring of my mind as I struggled to fix my issues.

I'd always thought I wanted the chance to set my own course. But now that the opportunity was here, the idea of finding a job I enjoyed, spending time with Paxton again, and moving to a new city was terrifying. The changes had happened with dizzying speed, and I worried I wouldn't be able to keep up. Yet, at the same time, anticipation sizzled through me. I might work for NASA. *NASA!*

And Paxton wanted to help me. We'd just…ended before, so I needed whatever this would turn out to be—whether that was closure or something more. I wanted the more, but that frightened me, too. I'd never had much of a support structure, even when my mother was alive. So I had to be realistic: my leg might well buckle when I took this leap of faith.

CHAPTER 9
Paxton

I was going to be in *deep* trouble with Coach for missing the flight back with the team, but I couldn't leave without talking to Hana again. Ida Jane had recommended that I give her time, but after seeing her with the skinny shit earlier today and the way she'd fled after the game, I didn't have that luxury.

I mean, I did, but I'd already missed years of time with Hana because of my father's meddling, and I refused to miss even a single additional moment.

That's how I ended up in the backseat of an Uber, my ear bent by a chatty driver named Herb. His nonstop dissertation seemed to posit that sports, women, and beer were the only necessities in a man's life.

Sorry, bucko, but we'll have to disagree on that one. "Thanks for the ride," I said, slamming the door shut when we finally arrived. He'd been entertaining and seemed like a decent guy, all in all. If I wasn't concerned about Hana, I'd probably have wanted to take him out for a beer or two.

I climbed the steps to her apartment building, unsurprised when a shadow peeled off the side wall. I eyed the skinny shit as he stalked toward me.

"You can have her." Skinny Shit sniffed as he strode past. "She's not worth the effort, and she's not even *that* good of an engineer. Good riddance to you both."

Why do people think athletes are divas? We're used to hard work and consistent, brutal rejection. This guy, though, hadn't worked for years on a singular goal—he didn't have the stamina for difficult tasks. Most people didn't.

"She's not a *thing* to toss between people," I told him, shaking my head as I tried to ease the annoyance out of my system. "Hana's her own person, and she'll make her own choices."

"Yeah, well, she can choose a different career as well, because I don't want her anymore," he sneered. "And what *I* say in aerospace tech goes."

Fuck. This. Guy. Gunnar Evaldson, the Wildcatters' owner, who'd made billions of dollars in his career, wasn't pathetically egotistical. But Skinny Shit couldn't see the damage he did to others because he was too busy trying to soothe his ruffled feathers. And the fact that he'd sacrifice Hana angered me. Even as I had that thought, though, I clenched my fist, hating that I hadn't behaved any better than him three years before.

But I was different now. I refused to be like Skinny Shit.

"Your loss, man." I gave him a wide berth as I headed up the stairs.

"She ruined the chance for a beautiful career—*for you.*" Derision dripped from his words, like poison from a snake's fang.

I kept walking.

"Men like you make me sick. Big, brawny—*stupid.* You just can't let the rest of us have something good, can you?"

"You never learned when to shut up, Jeremy."

I looked up to find the source of that voice and saw a girl

hanging out of the window above us. She waved. "You want to see Hana?" she asked.

"Yeah, if you think—"

"After Jeremy sleazed all over her earlier, she's probably desperate to see someone decent. Hang on. I'll be down in a jiff." She raised her voice. "And I called the police, Jeremy, for disrupting the peace *and* breaking and entering. And being a total creepy bastard who doesn't know the difference between a pen and his dick."

My new favorite person shot me a wink as I bit my lip to keep from laughing. Skinny Shit might have called me dumb— which didn't stick because it was ridiculous as well as wrong— but the woman above had just ripped his masculinity to shreds. I *liked* this girl. If she was a hockey fan, I was getting her tickets to some games.

She arrived, out of breath, a moment later. I noted her wide-set hazel eyes and thick, slightly frizzy coppery hair. An idea formed.

"Do you like dogs?" I asked.

"Yeah," she replied. "Who doesn't? Weirdos, that's who. So Jeremy must be a dog hater."

"How about hockey?" I walked through the door she held open.

She shrugged. "Never paid much attention to sports."

I heaved a gusty sigh. "Pity. I think you'd be great for my friend Cruz."

"I know Lennon, and I have watched him play a time or two."

I raised my eyebrow at her casual knowledge drop. The door

clicked shut behind us. There was just enough light for me to see her blush.

"I thought you didn't pay attention to hockey."

"I don't," she countered. "Really couldn't be bothered with something that has less meaning to the outcome of our species than the day's weather."

At my wince, she blushed. "Sorry, that was blunt. And rude. Erm…Lennon looked great in that milk campaign."

I smirked. "He really did. Made me want to drink some."

She giggled and shook her head. "Hana's place is that one." She pointed to a door.

"Thanks," I said. "Let me know if you decide you like hockey *or* Cruz. I'll hook you up."

She smiled more broadly, showing off a shallow dimple and dancing eyes. "Oh, well, then I should introduce myself. I'm Vivian Lee. But like I said, I know Lennon." A shadow of pain slid across her face even as she turned away to head back into her place. The door closed softly behind her.

Sucking in a bolstering breath, I knocked on the door she'd said was Hana's. I heard Hana's uneven gait move across the space, each step in tandem with my heart. She flung open the door, a scowl raking her brow.

"I told you never to come—oh, hello, Paxton." She cleared her throat. "Um, what are you doing here?"

I leaned my forearms on the door frame above us and enjoyed Hana's slight jaw drop and flash of interest. "Well, first, I need to make sure you're not talking to me about never coming back."

She shook her head. "No, that was my ex-boss." She hesitated, seeming to calculate something in her head before she waved me inside. I stepped into her place, noting that it was tiny but neat. Hana had always been tidy. That trait worked well for her here because the lack of clutter made the space seem…less tiny.

Her father's teapot sat next to the stove, and her grandmother's red silk coverlet was on the bed. Hana still wore her sweater and leggings, but she'd removed her boots and let her hair down so it spilled over her shoulder in a thick blue-black wave. I knew from experience that it would be cool and satiny to the touch.

"The skinny shit waited out front to tell me he'd fired you and I was too stupid to help you fulfill your potential."

Hana huffed. "I need some tea. Want anything?"

"Sure. If you don't mind."

"I'm making chamomile. Maybe it'll help me calm down."

She turned on her good leg and shuffled into the kitchen, the limp more noticeable. Based on how she favored her right leg, the left one had to be hurting. She filled the kettle and grabbed two mugs.

Ah, we aren't doing the full teapot, which means Hana isn't accepting me here for long. I understood, but I didn't like it. Still, I had to respect the boundaries she set. While I'd been duped by my family, Hana had been abandoned by me. I'd promised to love her, to care for her, and I'd walked away.

"What happened to the promise ring?" I asked.

Hana set down the box of tea. "I sold it."

I swallowed, unsure what to say.

She tilted her head and studied me. "That makes you angry."

I rubbed my palm over the back of my head. "It's just… I

worked for three summers to earn the money for that ring."

"And then you broke your promise to me, Paxton." The tea kettle whistled. "Look, rehashing the past is already tiresome. I needed to pay some bills. Especially…" She bit her lip and finished making us each a cup of tea. She set mine on the counter before lifting hers. Then she leaned on the counter behind her, making no move to close the growing gap between us. "Why are you really here, Pax?"

"Because I wanted to tell you again in person that I didn't know about the accident, the hospitalization." I swallowed. "The baby. And I'm so, *so* sorry you had to go through all of that alone."

She nodded. The steam obscured her a moment, and it felt as if I was trying to translate a language with no known vocabulary.

"Thank you. I absolve you of any responsibility."

I inhaled as I felt my eyes widen. "That's what you think this is? A way to assuage my guilt?" My jaw tightened.

"Isn't it?"

"No."

"Then what is this?" she asked.

She seemed calm, collected, but I caught the faint tremor in her voice. Hana was keeping it together, but she'd had a hell of a shocking day. If my appearance yesterday had impacted her like it had me, she hadn't slept much last night. Add to that the rollercoaster of today, and everything felt magnified and a bit warped.

Like I couldn't quite catch my balance.

I stepped around the partial wall that separated us and walked up until the toes of my dress shoes were inches from her leg. I bent my knees, which brought us much closer to eye level. "This is me, coming to you, telling you I made a terrible mistake. One I wish to rectify."

Those words cost me some of my pride. But what did that matter, really, if I was lonely and miserable? My pride wouldn't laugh with me or snuggle with me. I wanted that with Hana.

"I should have ignored my father," I continued. "Better yet, I should have told him to go fuck himself. I didn't. That's completely on me. And I'm so sorry you suffered because I wasn't brave enough and strong enough to be the man you needed or deserved."

My words seemed to bounce around the space before settling slowly, softly between us. Hana spilled tea on the counter, her hands unsteady. She set her mug aside and stared up at me, eyes liquid and warm, lips slightly parted.

"I want to be that man for you now. I know I have to prove myself, and I will. If you'll give me that chance."

"That's… Wow, Pax. That's a lot to process."

"The skinny shit told me about your job," I told her. I moved to the other side of her kitchen where it was wide enough for two narrow stools—the only dining space in the area. I nudged one of the stools out of my way and leaned my elbows on the strip of countertop.

She shook her head. "That's on me, not you. Jeremy…isn't mature. Or capable of not getting his way. And I'm sure many other things."

"Still, I dislike that you've been hurt because of me."

"Again, not your problem," she said.

I hesitated. "I want to tell you why I needed to get in touch with you, why I started to question everything my father told me—taught me."

She was still a long moment before she gave me a nod. "Okay."

I took a deep breath and returned to the day after Ida Jane and Maxim's second wedding last summer.

I'd woken in the dark, my eyes popping open as I gasped on a sob. I was a grown fucking man who'd lived alone for years, yet I'd cried in my sleep. I'd sat up, blurry-eyed.

"*Never drinking again,*" I'd mumbled. It made me vulnerable. Made me remember. Allowed my walls to come down enough to admit how much I missed Hana. Nausea had rolled through me, and I'd groaned as my head hit the wall.

I'd fumbled on my nightstand, found my phone, and called my mom.

"*Hey, hon,*" she'd sung out, chipper, when she answered.

"*I can't keep pretending I'm okay,*" I'd said.

"*Oh.*" Then, a quieter, "*Oh.*"

"*I miss her, Mom.*"

"*Oh, Paxton. I-I didn't realize…*" She'd sighed. "*That's not true. I did. You haven't been serious about anyone since you broke up with Hana.*"

"*Mom, it's killing me,*" I'd said, my voice low. "*I miss her. I ache because I miss her.*"

"*But…but you said it was for the best.*"

I'd snorted derisively. "*And whose idea was that?*"

"*I don't know what you want me to say, Paxton.*" She'd sounded upset.

"*I want you to tell me the truth,*" I'd told her. "*I can hear it in your voice. You know something."*

She'd inhaled, then blown out a breath. *"I'll fly out."*

"Why? Why can't you just tell me now?"

She'd remained silent for a long moment. So long that I'd been pretty sure she would tell me she'd changed her mind. *"Because this needs to be in person."*

"What does that mean, Mom?" I'd asked, my tone sharp.

Her swallow had been thick with emotion that I'd felt through the phone. *"It means that I—give me some time on this, Paxton. But you're right. You deserve to know everything. And the first thing I should tell you is that Aiki sold the house."*

I'd risen from the bed, propelled by the need to do something. *"What?"*

"They don't live down the street any longer."

"When did that happen?"

"I'll fly out," she'd assured me. *"We'll talk."*

"You need to tell me. Now. Starting with why Dad was so insistent I break up with Hana."

"I can't... I have to talk to your father."

"I'm going to get in touch with her. I should have done so sooner."

"Oh, Paxton, I'm not sure—"

"It's not your choice, Mom. It's mine. Clearly I don't have all the information, but I'm sick with missing her."

"You...you are?"

"Don't act like that's a surprise. You said a minute ago that—look, you saw us together," I'd said, my tone soft. *"What we had..."* I'd heaved out a breath. *"What we had was fucking special."*

I'd expected Mom to reprimand me for my vulgarity. Instead,

she'd surprised me. "*What you two shared was something most of the rest of us can't fathom.*"

"*Then why did Dad pressure me?*" I'd asked again.

"*Because you were young,*" she'd said, tears in her voice. "*Sean, it's Paxton, and he's asking…*"

The conversation had turned garbled, and then my father's voice had flooded the line.

"*Son.*"

"*Dad.*" I'd been stiff, standoffish with him since the draft. We both knew why, and it must have weighed on him as much as it did me.

"*I just… You were so young, Paxton,*" he'd said. He'd cleared his throat and continued, his voice gruff. "*Just over twenty-one, barely legal to have a drink. Heading into a career that was going to offer you every possible opportunity.*"

I'd gnashed my teeth at that ridiculous comment they kept making. As if I hadn't known my mind well enough then to know I wanted to play in the NHL. "*I would have thought you'd want me to keep my focus, and I didn't do that most of my first season, which nearly cost me my career.*" My tone had been accusatory.

I still couldn't believe my father had wanted me to break up with Hana, date others, instead of settling down.

"*You had your whole life to settle down, and I didn't think the girl down the street could be—should be—your whole life,*" Dad had countered, his tone defensive.

Mom had been sobbing in the background, which made the hairs on my arms and at the back of my neck stand on end.

"*That's not all of it,*" I'd said. "*You're still keeping something from me. Something important."*

Dad had sighed. *"Paxton, you have the opportunity to meet someone glamorous. Someone who will support your career, not expect you to support hers. Ending it with Hana was for the best. You know that."*

"No, I don't know that," I'd said.

"We're worried about you, honey," Mom had said. Her voice had been closer. No doubt she'd had her hand on my father's shoulder. They'd always been a united front. Always.

And in this, they'd kept something important from me.

"I'm unhappy that you're upset, but this is why we didn't want to tell you. We didn't see a way forward where we kept a relationship with you if we told you what had happened," my father had said.

"You're right. You don't. We don't have a relationship because you lied to me," I'd seethed. *"Don't call me. Don't contact me again."*

CHAPTER 10
Hana

Once Paxton stopped speaking, stopped relaying that horrible conversation, the silence stretched out between us, pulling tension tauter and tauter.

My heart thumped against my chest. "I don't know what to say to that," I told him.

"Once I knew you'd moved, I planned to hire a private investigator, but I didn't like invading your privacy. Thus, I kept putting it off, even as the need to see you, to talk to you, grew. It got huge, Hana. I woke up the other morning knowing I couldn't wait any longer. And then Cruz told me he'd found you. So I came out, and well, you know what's happened since."

"That's…" *Endearing. Shocking. An invasion of privacy.* I shook my head because I didn't know what to think, to feel. Everything was jumbled and messy, like when I'd lived at home. I hated chaos; I'd become an engineer to order the disorderly.

Yet turmoil followed me.

"Hana."

Paxton's eyes were full of emotion. "I would have come to the hospital. I would have been there for you."

"Thank you for saying that. But you weren't there, and I managed alone."

I was grateful for the half wall between us—it kept the

emotional distance better than I was able to on my own. Looking into his eyes, I wanted him to hold me, to reassure me that everything would work out.

Only life had proven that wasn't true.

"I think you should go," I said.

"I…" He blew out a breath. "I don't want to go. But I will because you're asking it of me. At least…at least let me talk to you—text if that's easier. Just…*please*, Hana."

I hesitated. "Okay."

Paxton nodded. "Thank you." He nudged his untouched mug across the counter. "I'll talk to you soon." He caressed me with those beautiful eyes before he turned and left. I sagged against the counter's edge and tried to get my emotions under control.

Didn't work. Never had with Paxton.

My phone beeped with a text. *Lock your door. That skinny shit may still be lurking around.*

That something that had cracked open in my chest this morning rose up again. This time I welcomed its warmth, even as I feared how much I wanted more of it.

～

Finding another job in Silicon Valley proved impossible, just as Jeremy had predicted—because Jeremy had made sure everyone knew he'd fired me.

"I told you this would be a problem," Esther mumbled, glancing around the coffee shop. "I can't be seen with you, Hana. Jeremy's put out the word that you're dirt, and, well…"

"What Jeremy wants, Jeremy gets," I confirmed. I rubbed my forehead, wondering where else I should apply. My savings were dwindling, and another student loan payment was due soon. I also had to make the payment for my hospital bills.

I calculated the expenses versus the amount of money in my checking account. Not good. And my savings weren't enough to let me cough up first and last month's rent on a place if I broke the lease on my apartment here.

My stomach swooped as I remembered Paxton's comment from the other night: "*I want to help you, Hana. Not because I feel obligated, which I do, I'm not going to deny that. But even more, I want to help because you deserve the opportunities. So, if it's money, a place to stay—you name it, and I'm there to make it happen.*"

Could I ask Paxton? *Should* I?

What choice did I have, really?

Pride was all well and good, but Paxton wanted to help, and he did owe me… Before I could change my mind, I dialed his number. Esther gave me a curious look, but said nothing, busying herself with her coffee.

"Is this a bad time?" I asked when Paxton answered.

"No, no, now's good. I told you—I'll make time."

I narrowed my eyes, listening. "Are you at the rink?"

"Yeah, but we're not at practice any longer. We're trying to get Adam—he played goalie for us for the last few years—to go home to his wife and kid."

I settled back in the chair and stared out the window. This conversation was easier, safer for my heart and wounded pride, than the one we needed to have. "Why wouldn't he want to do that?"

Paxton sighed. "It's complicated but not bad. Not really."

He told me more about Adam and Naomi's situation with their preemie son and a difficult dive into parenting.

A shadow fell over me, and I rolled my eyes as I looked up at Jeremy, who was now impersonating a TV villain by looming over me and scowling. Esther mumbled an excuse as she grabbed her coffee and fled the shop.

I didn't blame her. This scenario was ridiculous. My *life* was ridiculous.

"What do you want?" I asked, not bothering to move the phone from my cheek.

"Get off the phone and we'll discuss you coming back to work for me," Jeremy demanded.

"Hana?" Paxton asked. "Are you somewhere safe? I need to know that slimy worm isn't going to threaten you or hurt you."

"I'm okay," I said. I would have smiled at the worry in Pax's voice, but I was too busy studying Jeremy. I'd looked up to this man, considered him a mentor, my savior. I'd been considering a relationship with him.

But he'd used me. He'd turned my fears against me so I'd come to work for him. I saw that now—how I'd confided in him about my worries over finishing my last three courses and completing my degree, about finding a job that would cover my much-higher-than-expected expenses.

He'd used those fears to tie me to his company—to him, smug in the fact that I was thankful enough not to consider my other options too deeply. Options, I saw now, that he'd hidden from me.

Every time one of his colleagues had tried to talk to me about a potential position, Jeremy had swooped in and steered me away. The only time that hadn't worked was with one of Jeremy's investors—Gunnar something-or-other. He was a billionaire or gazillionaire who dabbled in petroleum, aeronautics…who knew what else.

We'd enjoyed chatting about the hinges and solar-based mechanisms designed for space before Jeremy had attempted to whisk me away. Gunnar had simply raised a thick, sandy eyebrow and said in that clipped, deep voice, "We were talking."

Jeremy had smiled ingratiatingly and said, "Of course, of course! But Hana gets tired—from her accident. I was concerned she needed a break. You do, don't you?"

And fool that I was, I'd let him lead me away, to a corner, tucked out of sight from Gunnar and the rest of the career-altering opportunities.

Now, though, after talking to Paxton and reconsidering my interactions with Jeremy from this new perspective, after dealing with the fallout he was willing to wreak to get his way, I realized something important: Jeremy wasn't a man. He *was* used to getting his way, which made him a man-child. That was the key to his personality; he acted entitled and got vindictive when he didn't get what he wanted. He had the worst qualities of personhood, and he held sway over many.

I wanted nothing to do with him and nothing to do with his world. If I didn't take this moment, make this stand, I'd be sucked back into the status quo and drown in disappointment and bitterness.

"Han?" Paxton's voice washed over me through the phone.

"You there? You okay?"

"I'm here, and I'm okay. Hang on a sec." I held the phone in my hand but didn't disconnect it.

Jeremy fidgeted, clearly less sure of himself since I hadn't caved to his demands.

"I'm not coming back to work for you," I said.

"You need me—" he began.

"No. Actually, you need *me*. And instead of treating me with respect like you would a different colleague, you threatened me and tried to coerce me into basically an indentured servitude."

"I pay—paid you well!"

"You paid me okay, not enough to get ahead with my loans. Not enough to move into a better place. That was intentional— yet another way to manipulate me. But guess what? Other companies can and *will* pay me better."

I didn't know who those people were yet, but they were out there. Like that mysterious Gunnar. Darn! I wished I'd talked to him longer, gotten his name…knew what company he worked for. I'd have to scour the internet.

Jeremy scowled, much like a child who'd broken his favorite toy. I hated that I was the plaything in the analogy. *I won't be again*, I promised myself. "I have a network outside of you," I told him. "From my undergraduate *and* graduate program."

I'd finished my master's degree a few months ago, taking advantage of an accelerated program for full-time employees. The hours had been insane, but I'd persevered, driven to complete the advanced degree so I wouldn't remain beholden to Jeremy forever.

"These are people who know me and also know you." I let

that linger. Jeremy might instill fear in his underlings, and even his colleagues in the Bay Area, but the country was large, and he had as many detractors as admirers, as I'd learned in grad school.

"You can yell and scream and belittle me all you want, but my record with your company as well as my record throughout my years at MIT speak well—and for themselves. You don't control me, and without *me*, you wouldn't have gotten as far as you have with the prototype. We both know you sabotaged the simulation, Jeremy. It won't be hard to prove that, either, considering I wasn't at my computer the entirety of the day."

"You'd leave your colleagues in a lurch? Now? When we're trying to secure such important funding—"

"*You* fired me, Jeremy. Explain that to your angel investors and your venture capitalists. You get to keep the prototype, of course, but it's all data that I understand how to replicate. *Me*, not you."

"That's not fair—"

"Do not speak to me about fairness, Jeremy. Nothing about the last few years of my life has been fair, and I'm not interested in your wheedling. We have nothing more to discuss. Now leave me alone." I dismissed him and put the phone back to my mouth. "Are you still there?" I asked.

"I am," Paxton said. "Remind me never to piss you off."

"You already did." I sighed.

Paxton was silent for a long moment. I ignored Jeremy staring at the side of my face. "If I could go back—"

"But you can't," I interrupted. For a woman who was taught to respect others' opinions, I was on a roll today with asserting mine. I liked this empowered version of myself. I liked her very, very much.

"What can I do, Hana? How can I prove that I want a second chance with you—at us?"

I'd pondered little else this past week, even as I searched for a new position. "I'm not ready to give you that yet."

Jeremy seemed to finally realize I was truly done with him, and he slunk off…for the moment. He'd probably be back with some even more nefarious plan that would make me want to rip out my hair. I had two more months on my lease, but it was time to pack up.

"I'm focusing on the *yet* in your sentence," Paxton said. "That leaves the door open."

I couldn't help but smile. I'd missed him. "I did call with a request," I said, the half-baked plan I'd played with a few times shifting itself into a full-fledged idea.

"What's that?"

"I'd like to stay at your place—while you're traveling—to meet with one of my former professors. He has connections at NASA. In fact, he took a position there as a team lead on the type of project I worked on here."

"You always wanted to work for NASA," Paxton said.

I did. It was my dream job, but because of my long hospitalization and difficult recovery—and pile of medical and student debt—I hadn't been able to consider a government salary. Now it seemed I might not have a choice.

But Houston cost less to live in than the Bay Area. I might need a car to get to work, but I could drive something older, as long as it was reliable. I'd need to practice, too, because it had been a while since I'd been behind the wheel. I took a deep breath as I considered the traffic and honking and freeways…

Maybe I'd find someplace close to the facility and walk. Walking was good for my leg, as it helped strengthen the muscles that had atrophied during my months-long recovery.

Yes, even with a lower salary, the move might work.

"I still do want to work for NASA," I told Paxton. "And I'm pretty sure I can get an interview."

"So you want to stay with me while you're in town?" he asked. The hope in his voice made me tense.

I hesitated, but it was important to be honest. "I figured I could stay at your house, maybe water your plants, while I had my interview. I'll be sure to plan it while you're out of town. That way, I won't be in your way."

"You wouldn't be in my way. And I'd like to spend time with you."

We were adults…friends, right? I could spend a night or two with Paxton, especially if the result was the career I truly wanted.

"What happens when you get the job?"

A smile bloomed across my lips at Paxton's use of *when* not *if.* I loved that he had that much confidence in me. I should find it in and for myself. "Then I'll find a place to live."

He was silent for a moment. "Just to be crystal clear, I want to ask you to move in with me and for you to let me love you, but I understand that I must rebuild what I broke."

Such a Paxton response. He'd always been honest with me. Never pushy, but always honest about his preferences. I appreciated that, even when I couldn't agree with his desires.

"I'm not ready to get back in a relationship with you," I said. "I'm not—Paxton, this is a bit confusing for me. I mean, up until last week I was sure you'd turned into the world's biggest selfish asshole."

He hissed a breath. "Because I acted like it. Damn, that hurts."

I could see his pained expression in my mind. I knew he was rubbing his fist over his heart. That I could have considered Paxton a selfish asshole showed how angry and bitter I'd become—with good reason. But I didn't want to be mad any longer. In fact, I wanted to find my way back to a friendly relationship with Pax. I'd missed him in my life. But we had to move slowly. I needed to be smart about this.

That didn't mean I planned to start something romantic with him again.

Yet.

Damn my mind for refusing to let me lie to myself. But it wouldn't.

Because I did still have feelings for Pax, and him coming here to tell me he had them for me was swoon-worthy and adorable and totally rom-com-movie-of-the-year perfect.

"My place is yours for as long as you'd like to stay," Paxton said, breaking through my ruminations.

Despite what my heart wanted—or maybe because of it—I dug deep and gave him the brutal honesty we both deserved. "I'm not sure we can ever rebuild our relationship romantically. I'm different now." I should have added that I'd been broken and stitched back together physically, as well as jaded emotionally, thanks to his leaving and Jeremy's betrayal, but those words stuck in my throat. I was a mess and mass of scar tissue, and I hated that.

"I hear you," Paxton said.

But did he? How could he understand what had changed if I didn't share those scars with him? If it turned out we got along well now, I would show him, I decided. But first, I needed to be sure I could trust him.

Staying with him for a couple of days would let me dip my toe in the water.

"I need to focus on *me* and finding contentment with my life before I even consider romance again," I said.

"I hear you, Han. You need time. And I have to show you I'm serious about missing you in my life and about us."

"That's not what I said…"

"It's what *I* need, too," Paxton said quietly. "Give me that."

I both hoped and feared he would follow through on the promise, pretty much my constant state around him, it seemed. "Let me see if I can get that interview," I said.

"Anything you need, Hana, I'm here," Paxton replied. "Don't hesitate or worry about the request being too much. Just ask me, and if I can make it happen, I will."

Well…my pulse sped up faster than laser thrusters as my heart melted. Now I didn't just need to worry about getting that interview. I fretted about holding on to my sanity. It was going to be nearly impossible not to throw myself at Pax if he continued to say—and follow through on—everything he was telling me now.

CHAPTER 11
Paxton

Hana wouldn't ask me for anything else. I couldn't imagine what it had taken for her to ask if she could stay at my house. I knew from the stubborn silence, punctuated by her soft, "Bye, Pax," that she was done being vulnerable right now.

She disconnected, and I stuffed my phone into my back pocket. I wasn't interested in talking to the guys anymore—not now—so I headed toward the rink's spacious gym. I selected a stationary bike, wanting to reduce the edginess the call with Hana had caused.

"Paxton. Nice to see you." Gunnar Evaldson, owner of the Wildcatters, smiled at me as he pulled a towel from the handle-bars of his bike. He patted his forehead as he continued to push through what looked like a grueling cycle of simulated hills. I had to give it to the guy—he was in great shape for fifty-something.

"You, too, sir."

"You appear to have something weighing on you," he noted. "Anything I can help with?"

Normally, I'd think that was a platitude, that the team owner wouldn't bother to listen to a player, but Gunnar was different. Hands on. Invested. Sometimes a pain in the ass, but always looking out for his players. In many ways, he was a better role model, a better man, than my father. I was thankful to be part of his team and hoped to play for the Wildcatters for many more years.

And I was thankful I had reconnected with Hana again. Because reconnecting with her was everything. Just thinking about her pretty almond-shaped brown eyes and lustrous skin made my heart patter.

How had I made it this long? It felt like waking up from an insidiously bad dream.

Gunnar still waited. I opened my mouth, shut it. Then opened it again.

"Does this have anything to do with your early flight out to San Jose and the fine Coach Whittaker slapped on you for not returning with the team?"

I winced but nodded, looking over at him. "Yes. I had to talk to Hana."

"She's the one who's involved in aerospace physics? Fascinating career. Very cutting edge."

I nodded again, unsurprised to learn Gunnar knew about Hana. "I hadn't spoken to her in years, and then when I did, she lost her job because of me."

Gunnar picked up his water bottle and uncapped it. "Hmmm...." He took a long swig.

Gunnar proved to be a good listener, which was why I backtracked and gave him more information about my father's disapproval of my relationship with Hana and his push for me to break up with her. Then I admitted that I'd screwed around and nearly lost my shot to move into the NHL because I'd been despondent and angry once I realized Hana was gone from my life. I pedaled as I spoke, but kept my leg work light since I'd already skated an additional hour at Coach's demand—part of my penance for not coming home with the team.

When I finished, Gunnar turned to look at his machine. I felt lighter without the weight of his icy blue gaze, and also after unburdening myself of the whole story—some of the guilt I'd carried seeped away as I realized I'd been a child who'd craved, sought out, and followed his father's advice. Doing so had hurt me, nearly irreparably. I would never again simply accept another's suggestion as the correct one.

"Silas and I talked about your situation when we offered you the contract," Gunnar said after a moment. He finally slowed his machine, and I noted the faintest of grimaces. At least the man wasn't a robot, as he'd seemed there for a bit.

He wiped sweat from his brow and took another long drink from his water bottle, leaving me to sweat it out for a minute. He held the power in our relationship, something a lot of professional players didn't like to admit. They had talent, acumen, and physical prowess, but they didn't hold the purse strings, and they didn't make the decisions that could take a team from average to Stanley Cup level.

Gunnar stepped off the machine, set his bottle aside, and leaned over, stretching. I continued my pedaling. "I know some people at Johnson Space Center." He raised his eyebrows. "You do, too, don't you, Paxton?"

"I've met with the public relations representative."

"And a team of scientists and engineers, who you're helping to translate their work into laymen's terms for the group of students you're bringing up there—what is it? Next week?"

I nodded, surprised Gunnar knew my schedule.

He stretched his other side as he continued to study me.

Of course. My trip to Johnson was Wildcatter sponsored and would reflect back on the organization. Good thing I enjoyed both kids and aeronautics. It would be that much easier to make a good impression.

"I'll make a call," he said.

"Thank you," I replied, though I wasn't entirely sure what he meant.

"Nothing to thank me for. You and Hana will have to hash out the details yourselves." He bent and picked up his towel and water bottle. "For the record, I like my players to be settled," he added. "I find that once they get into steady, long-term, solid relationships, their focus on the game is elevated." He waved briefly, turned, and disappeared.

He left me, still pedaling, to ponder that nugget of wisdom and wonder what I could do to prove to Hana that I would never let her down again.

Despite the seemingly positive step forward of discussing the situation with Gunnar, my nerves got the better of me that night, and I slept poorly. I wanted to talk to Hana, make sure she was okay, get her to promise to come to Houston sooner. But I couldn't push her.

She'd always had a backbone of steel. As quiet as she was, as often as people overlooked her for not being more assertive, Hana had a will of iron I could only marvel at. And now that she'd determined a new course for herself, I had to let her take it. Alone. Until—if—she invited me along for the ride.

Puck was at her stick now, and I must wait for the pass…or the pass over.

"What's up with you?" Cormac asked as I put my wallet and keys in my locker the next morning.

I stared at my phone for another long moment, noting its lack of messages, and sighed. "Nothing."

"Not nothing," Maxim said. "You dropped a serious emotional bomb on us yesterday—"

"I don't want to talk about it," I said.

"I get that." Cruz peered at me from my other side. His expression was kindly—at least I thought it was through the beard. "But we're here to listen. And to help."

"We were *awesome* with Adam yesterday," Stolly pointed out. "He and Naomi are solid again, thanks to our fabulous life advice."

Cormac shook his head in mock disappointment. "You offered nothing to that conversation, Stol."

"Shove it up your ass, Mac. I was on it like a freaking bonnet." Stol puffed out his chest and grinned. "I'm a relationship guru."

I glanced up at the guys. "Well, Mr. Guru, here's one for you: Hana told me she had a miscarriage after I broke up with her. I didn't know because, you know, I broke up with her and my dad got me a new phone. But yeah…I could've had a kid. One that's older than all of yours."

Cormac whistled, and Cruz shook his head, clucking. Maxim leaned forward, his thick biceps bulging and his pale eyes icy-sharp. "That's…fuck, that's a lot," he murmured.

He wasn't wrong.

"This is what's been bothering you for months?" Cormac asked.

I nodded. "Well, not the miscarriage but missing Hana and realizing I was the one who fucked up my happy, which, to point out, I had before any of you guys."

"Heavy weight to bear," Cruz said. "No wonder you've been melancholy."

"Who the hell uses words like *melancholy*?" Stol asked, cutting his eyes my way. He was trying to ease the heaviness I'd created, and I appreciated his effort.

"I do, pissant, because it's a good word," Cruz said. He looked ready to damage Stolly's pretty face.

"It is," Maxim said, stroking his chin. "I like this one. And it suits Naese. He's like the dude in that movie Ida Jane made me watch—the English one with the long, flappy coats and horses."

"*Outlander*?" Stol asked. "Millie's wild for that one. Loves the dudes in kilts."

"Keelie likes that one, too. I don't mind it because the sex is hot." Cormac's smile turned devious. "Wish there were more romance shows like that on TV."

Cruz rolled his eyes. "Off topic. We're fixing Naese's pathetic, melancholic life."

"Oooh, that's better usage," Maxim said. He repeated *melancholic* to himself and nodded.

Cormac laid his hand on my shoulder. "You cannot dwell on the past, or it'll eat you alive."

Maxim picked up the thread. "If you love her and want a future, you show her that. You tell her that, any and every chance you get." The words finished low, almost growly, which made him sound like he was threatening me, but that was Maxim: deep and murky, and one of the most thoughtful men I knew.

"Now what's going on with you and Hana—that's her name, right?" Cormac asked.

I looked around the group of us. Most of the guys were leaning in, clearly interested in this conversation. I didn't understand why people believed men didn't gossip or weren't fascinated by each other's love lives. I straightened my back and met their eyes. I wanted them to know I was fine with them hearing my business. I was ready.

"You talking to her every day?" Stol asked. He'd been in a difficult spot with Millie once, needing to gain her trust; he knew what he was talking about.

I nodded.

"And you're showing her you care about her feelings and thoughts?" Maxim asked.

"I'm trying."

"She needs to feel that you care about her," Cruz stated.

"I do care about her. I still love her."

"If anyone had told me we'd be talking *feelings* before a game, I'd have laughed, then hit them, then laughed some more." Cormac smiled. "But this is good—right, even."

"I've been telling you that for years," Cruz said.

"And I'm saying you're right," Cormac snapped.

And just like that, the easy, sharing moment passed as

aggression washed through the locker room and carried over into the game.

In fact, Cormac's aggressiveness rallied the team in a spectacularly dirty game that cost one of our second liners his eyetooth and left me with double black eyes after the Bruins' D-Man caught me at the bridge of my nose with his stick. The defenseman was ejected before Maxim or Cruz could pound him into the ice, which saved him a lot of pain.

I wasn't too worried about the slight cut and the swelling, though I was pulled from the game as a precaution in case of concussion. That left Stol working the offense with our old-timer who just wasn't able to get off the line quickly enough to hit the mark and take the shot. Still, thanks to my two goals before I was pulled at the beginning of the third period, we managed a three-nil performance over Boston.

And after, I had a concerned voicemail from Hana, who must have been watching the game.

"Please send me a text or call me—something—so I know you're okay," she said in that soft voice. I could hear the tension in it, and wondered if she was pacing her studio apartment as she spoke.

I called her back as soon as the game ended, even before I hopped in the shower. I wasn't doing any interviews tonight, thanks to my swollen eyes. Adam would drive me home, and Cormac would bring me to the facility tomorrow so the medical staff could check me out again. They might not clear me to play the next game. Everything depended on how quickly the swelling went down.

But before any of that, I had to reassure Hana.

"Pax! Are you okay?" she said in greeting. "Can you see? What happened?"

"I'm fine," I told her.

Cruz shook his head at his locker, mumbling about idiots and machismo. "Could have whimpered and gotten sympathy," he muttered.

I smiled, but I wasn't willing to lie to Hana. I didn't want anything but truth, respect, and love between us.

"Are you still at the arena?" she asked.

"In the locker room," I said. "The game ended about five minutes ago."

"Oh. Well, um, that was quick…"

"You sounded worried."

"I was. I am." She blew out a breath. "I don't know what to think—what to feel about you, Paxton."

"What do you want to feel?" I asked.

"Nothing."

I winced but absorbed her honesty. "That's…" I couldn't bring myself to say *fair*.

"That was mean, wasn't it? It's just… You make me feel, Pax. And I'm not sure how to deal with that—if I want to deal with that again."

Because of how much I'd hurt her. "I'm glad you feel something for me, Han. I care about you deeply. I worry about you and over you."

"Pax, I…should go."

As much as I wanted to ask her more questions, I knew not

to push. Not when I was on such thin ice. In fact, part of me swore I could hear it cracking. "Okay." I bit my lip, refusing to say goodbye.

She didn't say it either, not right away. In fact, the silence grew, and my heart fluttered with hope.

"If I call you tomorrow, would you let me know how you're feeling?"

I smiled, feeling like I'd just won the Cup. "Of course."

"Good. Great."

"Until tomorrow."

"Tomorrow," she agreed. "Bye, Pax."

She called me the next day, ostensibly to see if I was better. I wasn't, and I was in a foul mood because my left eye had swollen completely shut while the right one was a slit. My head ached terribly every time I moved, and chewing was impossible.

Hana picked up on my surliness because she asked if I had someone to help with meals, driving, all that important stuff I couldn't do while my vision was impaired.

I assured her that I did. "Mac—that's our team captain, Cormac Bouchard—will drive me in to the complex in a while. I'm sure I could ask one of the guys or the CATS to help me out with meals or whatever…"

"CATS?" Hana asked.

"Comrades, allies, teammates, and spouses. Gunnar created the term to use instead of WAGS—wives and girlfriends—to be more friendly to all types of relationships." I thought for a moment. "And because it's a fun play on Wildcatters."

"Yes, it is. Ida Jane told me about the CATS when I was at your game. I like that you're being inclusive." She was quiet again. With Hana, that meant she was processing. "But you don't have a...special friend who can help you?"

"Hana, I haven't been with a woman in well over a year. Closer to two. And it's a cliché, I know, but those reporters are there to sell copies of their magazines or articles or whatever. It's clickbait, Han, to highlight that I was seen with, like, four women coming out of a restaurant. And I think half those pictures are altered anyway. Just...trust me. I won't lie to you."

"I'd like to," she said. But she made no promise to do so.

I sighed. "What's going on with your job search?" I needed a change of topic, so I didn't grit my teeth and cause my headache to worsen.

"I called my former professor who's been working on the rover mission. You know, the one they sent to Mars."

"I've watched every video clip."

"You would." I heard the smile in her voice. "Well, he's talked to his team, and they're interested in meeting me."

"That's fantastic, Hana! Really great news."

"I know. I'm pretty excited about the possibility."

"I'll be rooting for you every step of the way," I said. "You know, I'm working with the Johnson Space Center. Working to build awareness of the need for physical fitness to take on some of these aerospace tasks like astronauts do."

"I didn't know that, but it's a good fit for you."

"If hockey hadn't worked out, I was definitely planning that direction," I said.

"I remember." Hana's voice was soft. "I promised to design your rocket so you'd be safe."

"I kind of wish that had worked out for us."

"Well, you get to simulate zero gravity, right?" she asked.

"Maybe. I'm not sure what they'll have me do. I'm bringing in a group of kids today—well, I was supposed to, but I can't because of my black eyes and the concussion protocol. Mira— that's my contact at the Space Center—is rescheduling the visit. I'll find out more soon."

Hana gasped. "Oh! I have to go! Dr. Gerenstein is calling me."

"Let me know how that goes," I said.

But Hana had already hung up. I tapped my phone against my palm, a thought forming. Would Gunnar involve himself *this* deeply in my love life? Was that the call he'd said he'd make?

CHAPTER 12
Hana

Nerves licked up my spine, causing my nose to twitch and my palms to itch. The need to win over this group of engineers and scientists pushed hard against my sternum. I pressed my hand there as I exited the rideshare and stared at the low-slung, unassuming building tucked into the lush greenery of Clear Lake, a suburb of Houston's sprawling metro area.

The pale-gray building was dotted with darker windows, and the thick asphalt parking lot overflowed with vehicles from the tiny Smart to enormous pickups. I was definitely not in the Bay Area anymore.

I headed toward the building, my breath shocked from my lungs as a blast of frigid air hit me when I stepped through the sliding glass doors. My leg brace dug into my thigh as I struggled to walk normally. I hated people to see my limp because it made some of them think my mind was also imperfect.

"Hi, I'm Hana Sato, here to see—"

"Hana?"

I whirled too quickly at the sound of Paxton's voice and winced as my leg muscles screamed in protest. I bit my lip to hold in the whimper, but I couldn't stop my eyes from filling with tears.

"Are you okay?" Paxton stepped closer, clearly concern. He cupped my elbow, fingers gentle.

His eyes looked better, yet both were still encircled with fading bruises. I wanted to touch the battered skin. "Y-yes," I managed.

He studied me for a moment, and I luxuriated in the warmth of his skin seeping through my cardigan and into my own. I'd missed his touch, his closeness. My leg pulsed with another throb, stopping me from melting against him.

I eased out of his grip, determined to stand alone. I'd been doing so for a few years now. Reconnecting with Paxton, even if we did eventually see where our connection took us, didn't mean I was willing to give up the autonomy I'd cultivated. "What are you doing here?" I asked.

He gestured toward the passel of small kids behind him, many of whom looked at me with expressions ranging from boredom to suspicion. "I'm leading this team of explorers on a space mission," he said.

The kids puffed up their chests, giggled…and remained bored. *Huh.* I remembered every one of those reactions from my own field trips. I'd always been giddy with delight because it meant more time with Paxton.

"And where are you going?" I asked a little girl who seemed to be following our interaction closely.

"To Marth," she replied. "We're going to thee the dirt and rockth on the planet by moving the rover. I get to handle the controlth."

"You and anyone else who wants a go, Laurie," Paxton replied.

The little girl's chin shot out stubbornly, and I shared a look with Paxton. She reminded me of me at that age.

A pang of loss hit me harder than ever before. If I hadn't

miscarried, I'd have a child. She or he would be younger than Laurie, but only by a few years. I blinked back tears and forced a smile. "Have fun with that," I told her. "And be sure to visit the Hellas basin."

"She said a bad word," said a little boy. He'd perked up at my comment.

"No, thee didn't," Laurie said. "Thee was telling uth to look at the largetht crater on Marth. It's called the Hellath bathin."

Laurie's lisp was as adorable as her big, bright eyes. How I wished I could hug her close.

"There she is! My star pupil! The woman of the hour!" Roger Gerenstein hurried forward. He wore an avocado green corduroy blazer over a white button-down shirt and chinos. His sneakers squeaked as they pelted across the broad expanse of the lobby.

"This is the brilliant mind I've been waiting for," he said, beaming. "Come in! Here's your visitor badge. Oh, and you've met our kids today. Good, good! They're getting a go with the rover. You should see Hana control that machine," he told them. "She has the perfect touch."

Laurie's interest sparked further. "Doth thee work here?"

"I hope she will," Dr. Gerenstein said. "We need more sharp minds like hers. And if you study hard, you might work here too, one day."

"We need to move along, Mr. Naese," said a pretty blond woman who'd been at the rear of the group. She offered me a tight smile and clasped her leather folder to her chest as she fluttered her lashes at Paxton. "We don't want to keep the kids waiting."

"No, we don't," he said, his lip quirking up at her obvious attempt to move him along.

Blondie bit back a gasp at his faint smile, and I turned away.

"You're still staying at my place tonight, right, Han?" Paxton asked.

I froze, unsure how to respond to his blatant claim to my time—to me.

"I…"

"Great," Paxton said, his eyes holding mine. "Ida Jane's making dinner. And Maxim wanted to ask you about the cable mountings for the space elevator. He's been reading up on the subject."

I offered a wilted smile. "Great."

"I'll wait for you—give you a lift. Save gas and the planet."

Oh, he'd backed me into a corner, the sweet jerk. "Great," I said again, already planning how I could sneak out—and not stay at his place.

"I'll be waiting," he said.

Those words landed hard on my chest, drilling into my heart. I lifted my chin. "I guess we'll see, won't we?"

Paxton stepped closer, and Laurie followed. "Yes, we will. Because I'll always be here for you, Hana."

He turned and Laurie mirrored his action, trotting to keep up with his stride. "Ith thee your girlfriend?" Laurie asked, her high voice carrying.

I winced.

"She's more than that," Paxton replied in his much deeper rumble. "She's my world."

"Thee can't be that, thilly," Laurie said with disdain. "You live on Earth."

Paxton looked back at me, his expression yearning. "That's true, but Hana's still my world. Both can be true." He turned and headed into a wide arch, lit by tiny pinpricks of light to represent stars.

I released the breath I'd been holding. Why did my body and even my heart continue to give Paxton Naese such a hold over me? He was going to break my heart again. If not right away, then once he saw my scars—or when a more fun, more beautiful woman caught his eye. That's what he'd told me before, that I wasn't enough for him.

I couldn't forget that lesson.

"Well, I see you and your young man are still together. How delightful." Dr. Gerenstein beamed at me from behind smudged lenses. "Let's head upstairs. The team's all assembled and ready for you."

I forced my grimace into a smile. "Great." My word of the day meant anything but. "Lead the way."

I really wanted to go to the restroom and adjust my brace, maybe splash some water on my face and give myself a pep talk. Instead, we were headed straight into the lion's den, and I'd have to hope I didn't embarrass myself.

I shifted my weight once we hit the elevator, thankful Dr. Gerenstein hadn't pushed for the stairs. He peered at me over the rim of his tortoiseshell spectacles. "There's a restroom to the right when we exit. I'd like to use it before we get into this meeting. If I know some of my colleagues, they're eagerly waiting to press you on the space elevator, so I'd recommend being prepared for a marathon session."

I blew out a breath and some of my nerves. "That would be great."

He leaned in closer as the doors opened. "Well, much as I wish I'd been the one to think about all this, I had an email from one of our patrons earlier today, and he told me to be gentle with you."

"Who?"

Dr. Gerenstein winked. "Well, now. If he'd wanted you to know that, he wouldn't have contacted me. Let's just say he's an excellent ally." Dr. Gerenstein ushered me off the elevator as I struggled to absorb the information he'd just dropped.

"He said you were the *real* architect of the project you'd been working on at Space Elevated, and he has grave concerns about Jeremy's leadership moving forward. In fact, he's recommended that NASA buy the company and roll it into our space program so the project can be completed—with you as team lead."

Nausea roiled through my midsection. Who was pulling these strings for me? Paxton? But how?

"Here's the restroom. I suspect your car accident left you stiff, so if you need to walk a few laps, just let me know."

My eyes widened. "Who told you that?"

Dr. Gerenstein had known of my car accident, of course, as he'd been one of my professors. But I'd tried hard to downplay my needs.

"I read the emails you sent me from the hospital, Hana," he said, looking at me evenly. "I'd hoped to meet with you, but you checked out earlier than you'd told me you would, and then you accepted the position with Jeremy—again, before I was able to talk to you."

The gleam of intellect sparked in Dr. Gerenstein's eyes, and I was certain he'd come to the same conclusion I had—that Jeremy had preempted his attempts to get me here, to NASA, a few years ago. Granted, then I'd needed the Space Elevated salary. Now, though, thanks to my diligence—and more years of penny-pinching—I'd be able to make a government salary work. Probably.

I'd figure that out because I wanted the job

"As you well know, the industry is small," he noted, "and I'd been pretty vocal about my desire to have you join us on this particular team, just as Gunnar's keen to have you join us now."

"Gunnar?"

Dr. Gerenstein tilted his head. "Gunnar Evaldson. He's the Wildcatters' owner and involved in Space Elevated... He said he'd met you at an event?"

"Oh...oh!" Gunnar, the man I'd chatted with before Jeremy whisked me away. He was Paxton's boss? I rubbed my forehead. That was a lot of coincidence. Had Paxton leaned on him to show an interest in me? "You're sure this is from Gunnar Evaldson? Not Paxton?"

"He's sure," a voice said from behind me.

I whirled too quickly and had to catch myself on the wall as my leg threatened to give out for a second time. I sucked in a breath as pain seared through me. *Dammit.* I wanted to be at my best for this meeting. And here I was, wracked with near-crippling pain. My own fault, all of it. I hadn't counted on Paxton being here or on Gunnar Evaldson, this eccentric, ice-eyed billionaire, to be interested in my work—my life.

Maybe he wasn't. Maybe he wanted to ensure Paxton was happy and focused. That made more sense than a bigwig being interested in me.

"Gunnar Evaldson," the man said, offering his hand. He wore a faint smile, and his eyes were the steeliest gray I'd ever seen. "I can't tell you how pleased I am to see you again, Ms. Sato."

I inhaled sharply as we shook. "Did Paxton put you up to coming here today?" I hesitated. "Did he ask you to put in a good word for me?"

"No. He didn't. And even if he *had*, it's *my* money and *my* time. I came to hear your interview, mainly because I want some answers on the ballast plans you created for the elevator, which I think show exceptional promise." He made a face. "And also because Jeremy Dorring refused to let me talk to you when I last visited Space Elevated."

I was acutely aware of Gunnar's sharp eyes as he stated that last bit. "I had no idea, Mr. Evaldson. I'm pleased to answer any questions you have on the design—as long as I don't break my nondisclosure agreement."

Gunnar leaned in a little closer. "Naese and I share an interest in space *and* in you, but I'm *much* more interested in space."

I had to chuckle at his bluntness, charmed by the man who might well hold my future—and Paxton's—in his large, callused hands.

Later that afternoon, I smiled at the group around the conference table as I finally leaned back against my seat. We'd talked for four

hours—four! I'd answered questions and limped to the white-
board, unconcerned about my impediment in my excitement to
share the details of my design and the potential it had for moving
goods into space.

The group of eleven scientists and engineers now rose to mill
around, some waving their hands in excitement as they discussed
parts of the design or its impact on space provisioning.

Dr. Gerenstein patted my shoulder. "Still as passionate about
the work as ever, I see. I'll walk you back downstairs. The team
and I need to discuss your potential employment."

He winked, which told me this was more of a formality than
anything else. Still, nerves crested through my belly and chest.

"I'll take her down with me," Gunnar offered.

He and Dr. Gerenstein chatted for another moment while I
collected my belongings and stretched my stiff leg and back.

Out in the hallway, Gunnar fell into step next to me, shorten-
ing his stride to match my own.

"How did you get access to this part of the agency?" I asked.

"A lot of money and the right connections," he said.

I nodded. I'd seen how money held sway, especially in scien-
tific settings. Experimentation was expensive.

"That was utterly fascinating," Gunnar said. I offered him
a shy smile. "I've never had anyone explain the physics so
succinctly. What's the end goal for this technology?"

I hesitated. "Well, clearly I'd prefer it be used to benefit
society as opposed to wage better war."

Gunnar chuckled. "That I can understand." He sobered.
"I'm the sole survivor of my parents' children. I had two older

brothers. One died protecting Sweden's interest in the Arctic Circle. The other was a hockey player, killed by a homophobe after the Swedish team's win at the Sochi Olympics."

I touched his forearm as he jabbed at the elevator's button. "I'm very sorry for your loss."

He pulled himself out of the darkness and blinked at me. "Yes, me, too. For us both. I shared that so you'll understand I'm not interested in more death or destruction either. But I am interested in sending carbon capture or methane—even heat, based on those reverse solar panels you mentioned—into deep space. That seems like it could help us win our war against the heating of the planet."

I shook my head. "It may buy us some time, but not if we continue our same behaviors."

We stepped into the elevator and faced the closing doors. "You're an activist," he accused. It was kindly, but still an accusation.

"I'm a pragmatist," I emphasized. "And the way we fix this problem is by changing behavior. You've heard the Einstein quote about madness?"

"Indeed. I like it because it's true. You cannot continue the same behavior and expect a different outcome."

"Which is why the work that NASA or Space Elevated or any of the many hundreds, possibly thousands, of startups looking to change our behaviors or at least extend the chance to change those behaviors is imperative."

"I look forward to debating this further, Hana," he said as the doors opened. We stepped out, and he gestured toward Paxton, who sat in a chair nearby, flipping through a magazine. "I think now you have a date with your young man."

I looked up at him, and Gunnar raised his eyebrow, as if daring me to deny my feelings for Pax. That had never been the issue.

"We'll see if he thinks it's one," I said, refusing to back down. I'd been cowed by Jeremy's position once, but I wouldn't let another man intimidate me.

Gunnar's eyes danced with mirth as he smiled, crooked and real—probably the first one I'd seen through the urbane façade. "I like you, Hana. I can't say that about just anyone."

"Your hockey players? The staff?"

"Mmm... No. They're a means to an end. Most of them I respect, and those I don't, I remove."

The ruthlessness of the statement was matched by the cold that had seeped into his expression.

"But I like you," he confirmed. "I'll be sure to tell Paxton so."

"Thank you, Mr. Evaldson. And for the record, the admiration is mutual."

He chuckled as he stepped forward to shake Paxton's hand. Then he leaned in and spoke into Pax's ear. Pax's eyes darted to mine. I waited, fingers laced at my waist, for Paxton and Gunnar to finish their moment.

Paxton gave a stiff nod and said *thank you*. Gunnar offered a wave as he headed out.

"That man is a force of nature," I said, staring after him.

"He thinks highly of you."

I refocused on Paxton, surprised to hear jealousy in his tone. I opened my mouth to correct him, but then snapped it shut again. *Let Pax stew.* He deserved to wonder, to be uncomfortable about my situation. "He's a nice man," I said, unable to hurt Paxton. "At least he was nice to me."

Pax nodded. "That's because he likes your mind. So much so he's thinking about creating a thinktank specifically so he can hire you."

I saw the uncertainty in Paxton's eyes, and my heart melted a bit. He was so confident on the ice. Even when it came to space, he more than held his own. Paxton had started his degree in astrophysics, and he'd made it through the first three years of the program before his agent had pushed him into the draft. Knowing Pax, he'd probably continued to take a class or two each semester; he wanted a college degree because he loved learning and experimenting. I was sure further education was in his future, and I could see him working for the space agency one day.

People might call him a dumb jock, but nothing could be further from the truth. He was brilliant both in mind and physical prowess, which was why I couldn't fathom his continued interest in me. I wasn't physically able any longer. The accident had taken something vital from me—my full range of movement. I tired easily, and I'd never run—let alone walk—without a limp. I was scarred.

"You ready to go?" Pax asked. "I thought you might want to drop your stuff at my place before we head down the street to Maxim's for dinner."

I nodded, though I contemplated my position as Paxton's guest and having interviewed for a position thanks to his boss, and how that made me feel, even as Paxton and I bantered during the long, traffic-choked drive.

"Houston's huge," I said, looking out the window.

"It is. Surprisingly cultured, too," Paxton replied.

"It's just so…"

"Everything," Paxton finished. "I know. You can find anything here—any food, any trinket, culture from all over the world. That is, if you know where to look."

"You like it," I said, surprised.

"It's grown on me. I've always liked the Wildcatters. I was stoked when they traded for me because I knew I was coming to a well-run and well-respected team. Gunnar cares about hockey more than most owners."

"Probably because his brother played for Sweden's national team."

Paxton shot me a look, eyebrows at his hairline. "He told you that?"

"Yes."

"You know more about the man than any of my teammates, then. And Mac's the closest to Gunnar of all of us."

"Let me guess: you're all intimidated by him."

"Of course we are! He's a billionaire! Our boss."

"He's just a man, Paxton."

"That's like saying you're just a woman."

"I am."

"No," he growled. "You're much more than *just* anything, Hana. You're smart, poised, beautiful. Hell, you have one of the richest men in the world playing your champion…"

I snort-laughed. "We have similar interests. That's all."

"Don't," Paxton begged.

"Don't what?" I looked over at him.

"Don't diminish yourself—what you're capable of, what you've accomplished."

I studied him, and the moment dragged out as tension—sexual tension—ratcheted up between us. I wasn't ready for that.

Paxton glanced away and accelerated, moving us forward three whole car lengths.

This time, I remained quiet as I stared out the window. I wasn't sure I could handle more of Paxton's thoughtfulness. It made me want him too much.

Eventually he turned in to a neighborhood with tall oaks that shaded the sidewalk and huge homes that sat back from the street. The pitched roofs done in slate or terracotta seemed to touch the hazy blue of the sky. Each yard was jewel green and neat, the driveways snaking back behind wrought-iron gates.

If we hadn't just spent over an hour bucking traffic, I wouldn't have known we were in the Houston city limits. I swallowed my shock when Paxton pulled into a driveway. The gate slid open, seemingly without even a remote click, and he drove up toward the large, white house. It had black shutters and thick flowerbeds that cradled massive trees. The front door was painted gleaming black with a brass knocker in the shape of... I squinted. "Is that a spiral?"

Paxton followed my finger and cleared his throat. "Yeah."

"Is that the Milky Way?" I asked. Ours was thought to be an excellent example of a spiral galaxy, in part because the Hubble telescope had been able to photograph it, so we had images to view—unlike some of the galaxies we believed to be hundreds or thousands of light years from ours.

"Yeah."

I pressed my lips together, unsure what to think. Paxton had the Milky Way galaxy on the door to his home. My focus, from the moment I fell in love with aerospace engineering, had been the Milky Way.

Today had been such a sea of emotions, with all the vagaries of an untamed body of water. I felt myself at low tide now, a bit laggy and unsure how best to proceed.

Pulling in a huge breath, I turned to face Paxton just as he parked his sleek, foreign sedan in the cool dimness of the four-car garage.

"I'm really confused right now," I blurted.

"Something I can help with?" he asked as he slid the shifter into park. With a touch of a button, he turned off the fancy car and faced me.

I gripped the edge of the buttery soft leather and swallowed, needing a moment to compose my emotions into words. "Loving you was easy, Paxton." I raised my gaze to meet his. His eyes were direct and guileless, showing me his soul, just as he used to. "I was completely unprepared for you dumping me."

I bit my lip as we both flinched. He opened his mouth, but I held up a hand. If he interrupted, I wasn't sure I could get these next words out—and they held the key to our future. If he really wanted one.

"You leaving started a chain reaction that I can still feel in here," I pressed a hand to my temple, then my leg. "You leaving is tied up with pain and fear and grief and…and being here, just sitting with you now, means that's in my head, warring with my mind about whether I'm safe and won't be hurt again. But the pain—not just my heartache over losing you, but what happened to my body—is, well, imprinted. And I want to run away, because right or wrong, I equate that with you."

My breath sawed out between my lips, and I blinked back tears. "I don't know if I can stay here, if I can be with you. I'm—this is a lot for me, Paxton. That's why I asked if you'd be gone. I thought maybe, maybe if I dipped my toe in, it wouldn't be as overwhelming. But I'm freaking out, and I…I…" The sob hitched my shoulders to my ears and bowed my back. I shoved my fists against my lips, not wanting to break down.

"Ah, Hana. Dammit. I don't know what to say. How to fix it."

I closed my burning eyes, no longer trying to fight the tears. "I don't know if you can. My mind is telling me to flee and protect myself. And part of me wants to do that, desperately."

He absorbed that a moment. "What does the rest of you want?"

I smiled, though it drifted away. "For you to hold me. To make everything better." I looked over at his tortured expression. "That's the whole knot. I want you even as I know I shouldn't. Even as my mind and body remind me of what happened when I did before. I can't express how much that accident changed me. It broke me, Pax, and fair or not, it's all tangled up with you."

CHAPTER 13
Paxton

Well, that was a skate blade to the chest. Not that I should've been surprised by Hana's admission. She sat there, her expression tortured and miserable, with longing calling to me from her brown eyes. And I ached to hold her, to fix the muddle I'd created.

I cursed my younger self, railed against my stupidity, all silently. She didn't need to hear my self-flagellation. She needed me to prove myself better than I had been years before. To put her first. To show her with my actions, every day, that she was my top priority.

That was much easier to say than to prove. Yet, I *must* prove it, probably many times, before Hana would lose that haunted look.

With unsteady hands, I unbuckled my seatbelt. "I'd like to hold you now. Please, Hana. I know I can't wipe away the past. I can only start here and prove to you that I'm yours, that I'll be with you every step of the way." I edged a little closer, and when she didn't shy away, I gently gathered her, holding her to my heart.

"Even when I freak out and am sure you're going to run again?" Her reply was muffled against my chest.

I hated that she asked that, but we were analytical thinkers. It was logical, and it was probable. "Yeah, even then. Because I love you, Hana. I do. I never stopped. I can't stop. It's part of me, like breathing. So if you need me to prove it over and over again, I get that. I respect it, too."

"I'm not sure that's fair…"

I breathed in the scent of her hair, nuzzling her scalp. "You and I both know emotions aren't logical. They just are. And if you need me to prove myself, I can do that. Hell, I probably should do that."

Her shoulders eased. "No, Paxton. I'm not testing you. That would be wrong. You don't deserve—"

I gave her a gentle squeeze, which caused her to stop talking. I pulled away from her warmth so I could meet her eyes. I cupped her cheeks, enjoying the feel of her smooth skin. "I want to deserve you. We both deserve happiness, fulfillment. How we get there will be our way. No one else's."

She studied me, those dark eyes taking in each nuance of my expression. "Do you think we can?"

Something in the way she asked, in the slight breathlessness of her voice, in the yearning that slipped into her eyes, made me sure she wanted that future as much as I did.

But this was what happened when you shattered something precious. It never slipped back together seamlessly. There was always work and effort—maybe blood and tears and cursing and the desire to give up already—before the beauty was once more whole. Though not the same, never the same.

But whole.

"Yes, Hana. We can," I told her. "If we work together. Talk to each other, open up to one another even when being vulnerable is like walking naked in a snowstorm…"

Her lips quirked up in a faint smile. I wanted to kiss her but held back. *Damn*, that was hard.

"Like you were willing to do now. That was fucking brave. I won't take you or your feelings for granted. Not ever again."

"Thank you." She shuddered out a painful breath. "You'd walk naked in a blizzard for me?" She giggled as I rolled my eyes.

"No. I might love you, but there are parts of me I don't want to freeze off."

She giggled harder, and I smiled. This, right here, this was what I'd missed. What I'd craved and searched for…

And found only with Hana.

Dinner was a boisterous affair. But we Wildcatters weren't known for being halfway kind of men, and our women were just as passionate and strong-willed as we were. How else would we manage to work together? We needed that strength of purpose to balance our own.

I stared into my iced tea as these thoughts swirled through my head. I was becoming like Cruz—a philosopher, a deep thinker. Losing Hana, which had been like amputating a limb, had created this more introspective part of me. I still couldn't understand why my father had pushed me to sever our relationship, but I knew now that his constant pushing had caused me deep harm. And that pain made me much more likely to stand up for what I believed in moving forward.

Never again, I promised myself as I looked over at Hana. She was having an animated conversation with Keelie and Ida Jane about tardigrades, of all things.

"She's a pretty cool chick," Maxim said. He'd scooted closer, ensuring that his words were for my ears alone. "I wasn't sure if she'd suit you, our crew, after she ran from Ida Jane. But I see it now. Her strength isn't in fighting back. It's in knowing when to retreat."

That Maxim had realized this almost at the same time I did proved I still had a long way to go on this Cruz-level philosophizing. "She's my other half," I told him. I didn't bother to lower my voice, because Hana deserved to know what I was thinking and feeling. I'd never hide what I felt for her, never try to bury it or make light of it again.

She stiffened a little as my words hit her, but smiled. I felt it warm my soul.

"Yeah, I can see that," Cormac said. He was across the table from me. He'd leaned back and laid a hand on his flat belly, his legs stretched out in front of him. He looked like an indolent ruler, except that he rubbed Keelie's arm with his free hand, seeming unable to stop touching her. "And I get it. Totally. When that piece clicks, the world just seems…right."

"Speaking of right, it's about time for our baby to go down for the night, and I need to feed him," Keelie said. She pushed back from the table and rose, with Cormac in tow.

Could Hana and I ever be that in sync? We had been once. Logic stated that we could get there again. Eventually.

I took a sip of my tea, needing the liquid to rinse the bad taste from my mouth. Patience wasn't my forte. I was a work-hard-get-results kind of man.

We all rose and said our goodbyes. Hana's eyes widened when

Keelie enveloped her in a hug, but she offered her cheek for Cormac's brotherly kiss, which she returned with a soft pat on his biceps. Then she turned back toward the dining area, a grimace cresting her expression even as she offered to help Maxim and Ida Jane clean up. Thankfully, Maxim had seen that look—and knew what it meant.

"We will clear up. You need to get off that leg."

Well, so much for the gentle suggestion I'd planned on.

"Is it bad?" Ida Jane asked. "I don't mean to pry, but I saw you shiftin' around and, well, I figure it must hurt…"

I held my breath, waiting. Hana gave me a contemplative look before she said, "It does hurt, pretty much constantly. Nerves were damaged, and they can fritz out on me, but the main issue is that I lost a lot of the connective tissue around my knee joint. For a while, saving it was touch-and-go."

"That had to be scary," Ida Jane murmured, eyes wide.

"It was."

Those simple words unleashed a maelstrom inside me. So. Much. Guilt.

Hana must have seen it, because she took my hand and squeezed.

"How did they save it if the tissue was compromised?" Maxim asked. He frowned at her leg, not paying attention to me.

I wanted to know the answer as well, but I didn't want Hana to feel pressured.

"There's a newer technique that allowed my orthopedist to add cartilage from a cadaver to my patella," Hana explained. "The problem was that the way my leg broke—at my shin near my ankle, then just below my knee, just above my knee, and at my pelvis—left me immobilized for months, which caused muscle atrophy. So this leg is shorter than the other."

"Ah. The limp." Maxim nodded. "But shouldn't the muscle tissue return with proper therapy and workouts?"

Hana chewed her lip, then shocked me by crouching and pulling up the hem of her wide-legged pants.

"You don't have to…" I began. But I stopped when I caught sight of the mass of pink and faded scar tissue that ran up and around her pale skin from the top of her boot—and probably lower—to the hemline of her pants, which now rested above her knee.

Maxim leaned in, studying. He tilted his head as he pointed at three separate lines of scar tissue around her knee. "These were the surgeries?"

"Some of them. Those gave me back cartilage and repaired tendons. But this is what I wanted to show you." Hana touched the longest scar, which ran along the side of her shin bone to meet the ones Maxim had been looking at. "Initially, the orthopedist put pins along this incision to reconnect the bone fragments, but it was splintered in too many places, so they had to go in and shore up the bone with more metal."

"Your leg is titanium, then? Indestructible."

Hana wrinkled her nose and dropped her pants back in place. "Definitely not indestructible. And not a superhero. My body continues to reject the metal they used. We've tried two different alloys. If my immune system continues to target it, they'll probably have to amputate my leg."

CHAPTER 14

Hana

Paxton had said hardly a word since I showed him, Maxim, and Ida Jane my leg back at their place.

I'd taken that risk because already, I could feel myself falling for Paxton again. He needed to understand the complexity of my health, how badly damaged I was. My leg was hideous—I knew that—but I hadn't expected him to withdraw from it. Disgusted, sure. I could understand that. I felt it when I looked at my leg, just as I also felt such gratitude to still have it, even on the bad days when it swelled and itched and burned.

We'd walked over to Maxim and Ida Jane's house because it was only a quarter mile or so, but Paxton hadn't seemed like he wanted me to walk back. I'd been just as adamant about using the two legs I still had. As a result, we'd walked most of the way in silence, and when he opened his door, I was exhausted. I headed for the couch and settled on it with a long sigh. Closing my eyes, I relished the faint throb in my leg. At least it was no longer a burning ache.

Paxton settled next to me and pulled my leg up onto his thick thigh.

"What are you doing?" I asked, opening an eye.

"I had no idea, Hana."

"I know. I didn't tell you."

"You could have died in that accident."

"I almost did. Well, afterward. I was in bad shape, not just my leg."

He laid his warm palms on my shin, and I moaned at how good that felt. He slid his hands up and down over my pant leg with just enough force to ease some of the tension in the stiff, overworked muscle.

"Want to take a bath? Would that help with the stiffness?" he asked.

"Maybe." I shrugged. "I don't have a bathtub, so I'm not sure."

Before I could say anything else, Paxton hauled me into his arms and started up the stairs off the entryway.

"What—why...?"

I couldn't finish my sentence. Being this close to Paxton—wrapped in his arms, settled against his chest—set off a wave of longing that hit me deep in my soul. I looped my arms around his neck and pressed my nose into the indentation at his throat.

"I'm taking you to my bathtub. It has jets. Those help ease my bruises, so I'm thinking it'll help with your scar tissue."

I loved how easily he held me. "Nothing's going to turn that skin supple again," I said. "I'll always be scarred."

He inhaled deeply and blew it out with enough force to part my hair. "I know that." He set me down gently in his bathroom, a wonderland of marble, glass, and brushed nickel. It wasn't as overly large as I'd expected, but I hadn't seen much of Paxton's house yet. We'd come in through the mudroom off the main entryway earlier, and he'd taken me up the stairs to the guest room. We'd left through the front door a few minutes after that to go to dinner, and I'd only made it as far as the first seating spot in the living room afterward.

I swayed on my feet, completely done in by the flight, the extended intellectual conversation at NASA, and my much more emotionally fraught one with Paxton this evening. A hot bath sounded decadent.

I clasped the cool marble countertop and watched quietly as Paxton filled the tub. Once it was a bit more than halfway, he turned on the jets, causing a thick froth of bubbles to form.

He gnawed on his lip as he looked at me, then back at the tub. "You look wasted. I'm kind of afraid to leave you alone to get in and get out."

I swallowed, nodding. "I might fall asleep in there," I admitted.

He hissed a breath. "I'll close my eyes while you undress, but I'm not leaving you alone, Hana." His voice held a layer of steel.

I chose not to argue. "The water's probably full enough," I said.

He shut off the taps, and while his back was turned, I took a moment to enjoy the lines of his strong back and firm, thick buttocks. Hockey players had the best butts in sports, no question.

I pulled off my cardigan and set it on the counter. Next, I began unbuttoning my blouse. Paxton stared, transfixed by the progression of my fingers, until I cleared my throat. He flashed a sheepish grin before he slammed his eyes shut with a muttered apology.

My blouse joined my cardigan in the growing pile as I flicked the clasp of my bra. My breasts were a good handful but not as generous as many women's. I wondered how they matched up to the others Paxton had seen. With a head shake and a sigh, I set my bra aside.

"What's that about? Something hurt?" Paxton's hands fisted but he kept his eyes closed.

Warmth seeped across my exposed chest and settled around my heart. If I received an offer and accepted the position here, I'd be able to be near Paxton…close enough for us to explore whatever remained between us.

Like he'd said earlier, for us to be healthy, we had to communicate honestly. So, though it went against my no-confrontation policy, I said, "I was wondering how I compared to the other women you've been with."

"Hana." His voice cracked. He tilted his head back and stared up at the ceiling. Even from this angle, I could make out the furrow between his brows.

"Strip down with me, Paxton," I said, shocking us both. His gaze flew to mine and held. I stood there, naked from the waist up. "Isn't that what this is? A chance for us to be vulnerable—naked with each other?" I licked my lower lip, and he tracked the motion. "I'm not going to have sex with you tonight. This is…too fragile between us. But like I told you before, I miss you holding me." My voice broke as I uttered my truth. God, how I missed his embrace. I'd never felt as safe as I did in Paxton's arms.

"You're sure?" he asked.

No. "Yes."

He kicked off his shoes while his hand went to the button of his jeans. I watched, awed, as he revealed muscled thighs under tight cotton underwear. I gulped, trying hard not to fixate on the bulge between his legs. He caught my furtive glance and chuckled.

"You can look at me any time you want, baby. I'm excited you're here, excited to be with you—in more ways than one."

I swallowed harshly as I realized he wouldn't—couldn't continue to want me once he saw the rest of my scars. I forced my fingers to undo my pants and unzip them, letting them pile around my boots. The brace was stiff against my skin, which cooled as the air hit it, reminding me again that I was not perfect like Paxton.

He'd bent down to shuck his underwear, so I knew the moment he saw my battered legs. The left was the worst—the one that had been crushed by the twisted metal, but my right leg had also broken, along with my left arm, which had a surgical scar just below my elbow where the doctors reset that bone.

"Oh, Hana," Paxton murmured. "What you went through…"

"I'm fine," I responded. But it was a knee-jerk reaction, given without any real thought.

"No, baby. You're not. And I just left." He scooted forward on his knees and pressed his nose to my belly. He wrapped me in his thick, strong arms, a palm between my shoulder blades and the other at the curve of my spine to the top swell of my buttocks. He enveloped me, made me feel warm and safe, and…

I choked off a sob.

"I'm here now, Hana. I won't leave you again."

With those words, the dam burst, and my sobs grew, turning thick and ugly, shaking my whole frame. Paxton whispered encouragement and words of love as he held me. The storm lasted a long time, and my head and eyes ached when it finally passed. My nose was stuffy, and I feared to catch a glimpse of my reflection. I must look hideous. I did.

Paxton met my watery eyes with his patient ones. He rose with a slight wince. He'd been on his knees this whole time.

"I'm sorry…" I began.

"Stop." He grabbed a tissue from the counter and blotted my cheeks before he swiped under my nose.

I was so stupefied by the crying jag and by the way he cared for me that I let him. *I let him.* "I should go…" I couldn't think straight. My head hurt. My heart hurt. My leg hurt.

"Into the tub with you, baby." Paxton tossed the tissue in the trash can next to his sink and hooked his thumbs into my panties. "Okay?"

Was it? Paxton had just held me through a crying jag, naked on his knees. He stood before me now, big and sturdy and calm. I forced myself to nod.

This might be metaphorical—maybe even silly—to be physically naked together. But I needed him to expose his vulnerability, like he'd said.

He slid my panties down my thighs, and his fingertips left a trail of warmth in their wake. I shivered, and he chuckled with dark intent. At my feet, he removed my shoes and ankle socks, then my pants and undies. I stood before him in just my leg brace.

He touched the brace where it latched above my knee. "Does this need to come off?"

I nodded even as I brushed his fingers aside and undid the clasp. I grunted as the full weight of my leg hit the ground without support. Paxton swept me into his arms and then into the warm, frothy water in the tub, settling behind me. He used his long leg to flick the hot water tap open.

"Got too cool," he said against my ear. He held me close, my bottom nestled to his crotch, as the water warmed and the tub filled to dangerous levels. He nudged my left leg upward until my knee was positioned right at one of the jets. My head dropped back, and my back arched, shoving my rear end tighter against his lap as the water hit a sore spot.

"Good?" he rasped.

Yes. I could feel his growing interest in my wet body pressed against his. I nodded, too focused on the tension building, building, building in my thigh…

With another moan, I sagged back against him as the discomfort eased. I whimpered, shocked by how similar that release had been to an orgasm. I settled my cheek against his shoulder, my nose pressed into his neck, giving Paxton control over my body.

And it felt *right*. As it was supposed to be.

Which was when I realized my mind had been fighting my heart since the moment I heard his voice in the hallway of Space Elevated all those weeks ago. I was in love with Paxton. Like he'd said, I always would be. He was a part of me; we'd connected that first time we met, when he was eight and I seven years old, and nothing, not even his leaving me, could make me stop.

He held me securely, and I let myself drift in the safety of his embrace.

"If you get the job at NASA, you should move in with me, Hana."

"What?"

"Move in with me." His lips brushed across my brow. "I don't want to be apart from you again—any longer. We can be roommates, if that's what you want, need. As long as you're here with me, I'll be happy."

"I…" The tension crept back into my loosened muscles. "That seems fast."

"I've known you for seventeen of my twenty-four years. I've loved you for each of those. Nothing about this is fast or without lots of consideration. I'm not asking you to fall into bed with me, though I would love to worship you, believe me."

"I'm not ready for that."

"Why?"

He hadn't asked because he expected me to fall into bed with him. He was asking because he wanted me to elaborate on my answer, which I didn't want to do. I pulled in a breath from between my teeth. "Because I'm not sexy. Or beautiful like the women you've been with—"

He flipped me over so quickly, I didn't even have time to gasp. We were nose-to-nose, and his gaze burned into mine.

"You, Hana Sato, are the love of my life. You're beautiful, smart, funny, and fun. No one else compares. *Could* compare to you." He waited, his eyes slightly narrowed as if daring me to argue.

"The water's overflowing the tub," I said.

He cursed and flipped off the tap, then used the same foot to open the drain. I studied him, considering his offer— gobsmacked to find I was considering his offer.

He seemed to feel my inspection and returned my stare boldly. "Stay with me," he said again. It was a demand but also a plea.

"I need to get the job first," I said. *And I need to know that you mean what you've said. I want to believe you. Paxton, please don't play games with my heart. I'm not sure I can handle a second heartbreak.*

The pain of Paxton leaving me the first time mixed again with the agony of my broken body, my brother's screams, my mother's blood.

"You will."

I blinked, the nightmare my mind had recreated faded away, and I gripped Paxton's slick skin under my hands, grounding myself. A ripple pulsed up my spine as I tried to calm my racing heart. I tried to avoid those memories; they left me clammy and wiped out. "We'll see," I finally told him.

"I'm holding you to that," he said as he gathered me even closer.

I loved how he cradled me, enjoyed the feeling of peace that permeated the safety of his embrace, yet I couldn't *quite* bring myself to relax fully against him again.

The pain and fear had burrowed deep into my psyche, possibly too deep for me to root out.

CHAPTER 15

Paxton

Hana was holding back. I could feel it in the vague stiffness of her spine. Frustration oozed from my pores, but I reminded myself I must be patient. Trust wasn't fixed in a day, a week…a month.

Still, I fizzed with the need to…*what*? Force her to love me as I did her? That wasn't possible.

With a heavy sigh, I loosened my arms. It felt like I was giving up on her, on us, but I'd said what I could, done what I could… for now. Hana needed to decide if she was willing to take the next step.

Unable to handle being this close to her another moment, I pushed from the water, sloshing some on the floor. I grabbed a towel and wrapped it around my waist.

"Stay in here as long as you like," I muttered. "I'm going to pack."

Hana threw an arm over her chest and pressed her thighs together. I gritted my teeth as I turned on my heel and left the room.

So much for making progress. She was hiding from me. That was even worse than her defiant attempt to disgust me with her injuries. Good thing I had an early flight tomorrow, because every interaction between us scraped my nerves raw. I knew I was to blame, but I hated the distance between us.

I calmed once I'd dressed in pajama pants and a T-shirt. I finished my packing, an ear out for Hana's movements in the tub. I heard the water drain and her faint splash.

When I heard her grunt of pain, I laid the pair of slacks I'd folded on top of the others and poked my head around the corner. Hana leaned against the edge of the counter, wrapped in a towel. I took my time tracing each red scar, memorizing them, trying to grasp the enormity of her injury and subsequent surgeries.

I sucked in a breath when she leaned down and rubbed the deepest scar, her face contorted with agony.

She still hurt. Maybe she always would. And that pain would be a reminder of me turning my back on her. My stomach flipped as I realized I was hoping for a miracle to have her move toward reconciliation at my pace. She was still dealing with the fallout of my choices, and always would be.

The next morning, I turned from my blender and was surprised to find Hana lingering at the edge of the kitchen. She looked past me toward the ornate three-oven French range that sat proudly in the custom alcove I'd had designed for it.

Her hand fluttered up to her chest, her fingertips touching her blouse over her heart.

"Morning," I offered as I switched off the blender. "Sorry if the noise woke you. I'm leaving in twenty minutes, so you'll have plenty of time here without me."

She had to tear her eyes from the range. She licked her lips, opened her mouth, shut it, and licked her lips again.

She refocused on the appliance. I poured my smoothie into a glass, grimacing at its healthiness. I hated green smoothies with a passion, but I drank one every morning because the team nutritionist wasn't happy with my vegetable intake, and this was the fastest way to get the largest number of the bitter greens into my system as possible. I hated to admit it, but I loved how energetic and supple my muscles felt after drinking sixteen ounces of gross.

"Y-you remembered." Her voice trembled.

I'd just gulped the biggest mouthful possible. I swallowed, grunted at the taste, and set the glass down. "There's not a thing wrong with my memory, Hana." I was surly from poor sleep, disappointment, and my unpalatable breakfast. To prevent myself from saying something stupid, I picked up the smoothie and downed the contents.

"I just...I can't believe...that's my dream range."

I shoved the glass under the tap and rinsed it out. "I'm aware."

"Why?"

"Why what?"

"Why did you buy it?"

"Because I have a multimillion-dollar house, and that stove increased its value."

She padded closer and laid her hand on my tense forearm. "Paxton."

I sighed, forcing the bad mood out with my hissed breath. "I bought it for you," I admitted. "I wanted to be close to you. Wanted some connection. It's *ridiculous*, but since I couldn't have you—"

"You bought the thing I most talked about, most dreamed of."

I nodded because she already knew that.

"Have you used it?" she asked breathlessly.

"I can't cook."

"Still?" She tipped her head back to look at me, and her long hair cascaded over her shoulder, tickling the bare skin at her elbow. She had faint, tiny scars there. From shattered glass, I'd bet.

Without thought, I brushed the hair away, my fingers lingering on her warm skin. If things were different between us, I'd pull her close, nuzzle my nose into her hair, kiss her soft skin, her lips.

"You've never used this beauty?" Hana gasped.

"No."

"Pax—"

"It's for you," I said. I shook my head and sighed, deflated. There was no point holding back because I wasn't sure I'd get another chance to say any of this to her. "The house, the move to Houston to be near NASA, the fancy range, even the bathtub in the master bedroom. I was thinking about you every step of the way. I bought this place and made the renovations from the list you'd created for your dream house."

"You hadn't talked to me—"

"Because I was terrified." I stared up at the ceiling. "How could I beg for the forgiveness I didn't deserve?"

"But, but you did all this…" she sputtered.

I tipped my chin down and stared at her. "You don't get it." Emotion clogged my throat. "You're *in* me, a *part* of me. I can't look at a regular fucking stove and not hear your comments about the best one on the market. I can't not want to give you the biggest, best walk-in closet that is pathetically empty because I

don't give a shit enough about my own appearance to fill it up."
My chin wobbled, and I wanted to bawl out all the feelings I'd
held in since I turned my back on her three years ago. "I'm sorry.
I know that's not enough. I know it doesn't fix what I broke. I
know you're holding back."

She opened her mouth but then shut it. We both knew that
was true. I understood her reasoning, though I hated the reason
for it.

"You have to understand, Hana. I may have left you, but you
never left me. All I want is to hold you and be your sous chef like
we joked about and make all the hard feelings and this terrible
gap between us disappear so I can go back to loving you with the
lighthearted ease I didn't know how much I'd miss."

I moved away, giving her time to process and myself time
to regroup from the latest emotional bomb. My bag was at the
garage door; I headed toward it, calling back over my shoulder,
"Enjoy your stay. I'm back in two days. I hope you'll be here. And
I'll text you later."

Walking out this time was both harder and easier.

At least I'd had my say.

CHAPTER 16
Hana

If I hadn't seen the longing in Paxton's expression, I would have assumed something stupidly terrible like he'd found my scars too hideous and couldn't wait to get away from me. But that wasn't what I saw, and what he said...I was slowly beginning to accept.

I was still standing in the same spot, working through Paxton's comments when the garage door opened again, and minute later a friendly, feminine voice called out, "Hello!"

Who the hell was at Paxton's place at seven thirty in the morning?

Ida Jane poked her head around the corner, her blond hair nearly as shiny as her smile. "Good! You're up. Maxim left me the hulking beast of a vehicle so we can go shopping. Tell me, what's your budget?"

I blinked at her, my mouth slightly parted. These people didn't communicate on my plane. *Budget? Shopping?* "What?"

"Paxton said he'd invited you to move in here, and I'm sure you plan to make it look less like a..."

"College dorm room?" I asked with a wrinkle of my nose. I turned toward the sparse living room furnishings, all facing the nearly cinema-sized flat-screen TV.

"I think it's crazy because he made such an effort in the kitchen, and then he refused to let me use that gorgeous machine." Ida Jane looked longingly at the French range I'd just freaked out over. "At least he has a nice bedroom," she added.

If I believed what Paxton said—and I did; so help me, I did. Still…this was all moving too quickly. My head spun, and I couldn't gain firm emotional footing. I needed more time to process, to consider my options.

"I'm not sure moving in with Paxton is a good idea, even if I were to get the job with NASA. And, well, Paxton built out the kitchen based on a silly scrapbook I put together in college."

Ida Jane shook her head. "That is *terribly* romantic. Damn these huge, burly specimens of athletic prowess for being so sensitive." She shot me a sly glance. "Want to start up that range? We could make a feast."

I smiled as I shook my head. "The first time it's used, Paxton needs to be here."

"Ah! I knew it," she crowed. "You plan to come back."

"I…" I twisted my fingers together.

"Tea," Ida Jane mused. "It's more soothing than coffee, and Paxton said you prefer it. Then I think I need to gather the troops. Millie, Naomi, and Keelie will want to be here for this big reveal you're just dying to share. Don't worry, they've all been through something similar." Ida Jane moved through the kitchen like she'd been here before, and I swallowed the stab of jealousy.

Paxton had spent multiple years living his life without me, just as I… "I always expected him to come back," I said. I blinked in shock at those words I'd never let myself dwell on. I slammed my mouth shut, unwilling to say more.

Ida Jane looked up at me as she set the mugs on the counter.

"What kind of tea do you want?"

"I'm not sure." I moved closer and looked around. With faint annoyance, I asked, "Where are the options?"

Ida Jane's eyes sparkled as she led me to a pantry-style set of cabinets. She opened the top two doors, and I gasped in dismayed delight.

"He went to the tea store when he found out you were coming to town."

"And bought every single tea they had—"

"Except Earl Grey because, and I quote, 'Hana doesn't like it. She thinks it tastes like a dirty sock and moldy orange'," Ida Jane noted.

I giggled as I shook my head, my eyes never leaving the treasure trove of teas. There were boxes and boxes of them lined up neatly.

"This must have cost a fortune," I murmured.

"It sure did," Ida Jane chirped. "Pick something yummy for me, too. I'll get the CATS over. We have some deep emotional work to do before the retail therapy."

I looked over my shoulder. "I don't really have the budget—"

Ida Jane's scoff cut me off. "Paxton gave me his card. We're going to smoke that sucker." She grinned brightly as she clicked on the electric kettle. "Tea. CATS. We got stuff to do, my friend."

Once they were all gathered around Paxton's saw-milled maple kitchen table—also something I'd added to my dream-house scrapbook—I told the women the story of me and Paxton, mainly because I was tired of trying to shoulder the burden by myself. When I got to him breaking up with me, all four of them sat forward, eyes wide.

"Asshole," Keelie muttered.

"Shh!" Naomi said, waving her hand.

"You're right, Kee," Millie said, bumping her friend's shoulder. "That was a douche move."

"Shh!" Naomi said more forcefully. "I gotta hear the next part."

I offered a faint smile and launched into my teary, sleepless night and the realization that I should talk to Paxton. Then came the photos of him partying with all the women at that bar. So I explained that I'd done what I never had before: I'd called my mother for support. She'd insisted on picking me up, which surprised me. I was even more shocked when I realized she'd brought Aiki.

In the car, she'd told me I should consider taking a trip—right in the middle of my semester. That she'd packed a bag for me, and I could visit my father's relatives in Tokyo. Then I'd realized Aiki was driving strangely, and I'd tried to stop him. He'd ignored me, sped through a red light, and smashed into oncoming traffic.

"You didn't know he was on something?" Ida Jane asked.

"I had no idea my brother was high when they showed up. *None.* If I had, I wouldn't have gotten in that car, and I wouldn't have let my mother ride with him. For the record, Aiki being moody and surly was pretty much expected."

I stared down into the dregs of my tea. I'd tried an herbal blend meant to soothe and relax. I wasn't sure it had worked, but it tasted delicious. "Because he was high, he was cited for that and a slew of other things besides just causing the accident.

Between his bills from the accident and my medical bills from the doctors patching me back up, we had to sell the house. He made that decision while I was still in the hospital. It would have been okay, I guess, but he used all the money for his legal defense." Once again proving I couldn't rely on the men in my life.

"Do you miss the house?" Naomi asked.

I shook my head. "My only happy memories there involved Paxton."

"Which brings us back to the gazillion-dollar question," Millie said. "Why did his father push him so hard to break up with you?"

I tilted my head. "I've wondered that, too. Mr. Naese was always kind to me, if a bit disinterested. Though I did hear him ask Pax once why he wanted to spend his free time with me and not at the rink."

"Ah. One of *those* dads," Millie said with a curl to her lip. "I hate the controlling ones the most."

"As you should," Ida Jane agreed, patting her shoulder. "Millie can tell you about her horrible dad after we get to the bottom of this muddle."

I shook my head. "There isn't a muddle. Paxton broke up with me, I broke, literally, and now he wants to make amends, possibly try for another shot as a couple since he hasn't been able to find what he's looking for in another woman." If I believed what he said, that wasn't exactly true of his motivation. But close enough for now.

Naomi wrapped her arm around me and laid her head on my shoulder. The comfort was as shocking as the familiarity. "Sometimes you have to shatter. We aren't meant to bend and twist forever. And *sometimes* that break makes us stronger."

"Not until we manage to pick up the shattered bits, though," Millie said. She launched into her history and how hard it had been to lose her mother, live with her father, and how little she'd trusted Luka when he came into her life.

"I'm here to tell you good things can happen again, especially after the pain. I think—though Ida Jane can probably speak to this better—that sometimes you need that valley, that ultimate low, to understand just how wonderful the love you're being offered is."

I shoved back from the table, antsy with emotion. "But Paxton and I were in love back then. We had our future mapped out. We were *happy*." My lower lip quivered but I firmed it. No more tears. I hated that I'd broken down with Pax last night, even though I knew I'd needed that release.

I met the gaze of each of the women sitting at Paxton's table— the very one I'd seen in the Amish furniture shop I'd dragged him into on that weekend we'd slipped down to Pennsylvania during my sophomore year of college.

"Happiness doesn't last," Ida Jane said. She smiled kindly. "It's an *emotion*, which means it changes. Stressors pushed you two apart for a reason—"

"Exactly!" I exclaimed.

"Can you honestly say you're not interested in Paxton? That you don't find him sexy?" Ida Jane raised an eyebrow. "That you weren't envious that I knew my way around his kitchen better than you?"

The women smirked and leaned back. Irritation swirled through me, but like a dust devil, it dissipated as I stared at their open expressions. They weren't pushing me into Paxton's arms, but they sure did bring a whole bucketload of truth, which I'd intentionally pulled back from last night with Paxton.

They wouldn't let me hide because they knew, in the long run, I'd hurt myself more by doing so. With a jolt, I realized *this* was what it was like to have close friends. Besides Paxton, I'd never had this community before. And they'd accepted *me* because they loved *him*.

I sucked in a breath past my achy throat. "I want him. I can admit I still love him, which he knows. And he's told me he loves me, too." I resettled in my chair and stared down at my tightly clasped hands.

I jolted when Naomi laid her tanned hand over mine. "But sometimes love doesn't feel like it's enough," she said. "Or it feels like a prison. Right?"

I gave a brief nod.

"Because you don't have the trust to back those feelings up," Ida Jane said.

"And without the trust," Keelie added, leaning closer so that she, too, could clasp my hand, "you're flailing in the wind. Scared out of your mind. At least I was."

"As a smart lady once told me, that's why they call it *falling* in love," Millie said.

"It's a leap over a seemingly huge, empty chasm," Naomi said.

"But if you don't give yourself the opportunity to let trust grow and flourish, you'll stay here, in this horrid limbo," Keelie said. "It's the absolute worst place, even if it does feel safe right now."

Huh, she got it, too. From the sadness in her eyes, I knew

she'd had her own fears, which continued to linger despite her obvious happiness with Cormac.

"It takes strength to move forward," Ida Jane said. "But it's also the only way out of the…" She pursed her lips, clearly seeking a good metaphor.

"The shit river at the bottom of the hell valley you find yourself in," Naomi said.

We all gaped at Naomi, who calmly sipped her tea, then smacked her lips.

"Such a way with words," Millie said before she snorted a giggle and we all burst into hysterics.

CHAPTER 17

Paxton

Hockey proved a relief for my frustration about the situation with Hana. From the moment Stol slapped the puck my direction after winning the face off, I was in the zone. I raised my gloved hands in the air after scoring a third goal deep in the second period and ended up mobbed by my teammates. We were up by four over the team considered our biggest rival for the championship.

Coach Whittaker pulled our line early in the third, and I drank deeply from my water. As I set the bottle down, I studied the crowd. I felt my eyes widen as my parents waved to me. My mother looked tentative, but my father was his usual confident self. He shot me a double thumbs-up and a big smile.

I looked away. Seems they hadn't believed me when I'd told them I was done, so they'd showed up at one of my games, just like they had off and on for my entire hockey career.

The itch to know where I stood with Hana grew, and by the time the final buzzer sounded, I'd lost some of my enthusiasm for our big win.

"Great game, man," Cormac said, patting my helmet with his gloved hand as we trudged down the hallway toward the visitors' locker room. A thick rubber pad protected our skate blades and kept us out of the melted ice that dripped from our gear.

"Thanks."

"What's with the grumpiness?" Stol asked. He elbowed my side, and I grunted as I scowled. "Definitely grumpy."

"My parents are here," I told him. "They're going to insist I talk to them."

"This about your girl?" Maxim asked.

I shrugged. "I'm not sure she's mine." I sighed. "She's not ready to commit."

"Considering she spent the day with our wives, I'd have to say she's one of us," Maxim replied.

"She did?"

Cormac nodded as he began to strip off his gear. "Keelie sent me photos of their shopping excursion. Hope you're prepared for that bill."

Stol grimaced. "I've heard Adam complain about Naomi's trips to Nordstroms."

"Whatever, dude. Your wife is way more loaded than you," I shot back.

He shrugged. "Until she figures out how to divest herself, sure. But she doesn't want that weight for Bree."

"Weird that you're trying to get rid of what most people covet," Cruz said from his locker. His hair was a mess, and he had dark circles under his eyes. He looked unkempt and exhausted, and I understood completely. That made me wonder if *he* was having relationship problems. But…that couldn't be right. He'd said his woman was dead and buried.

"Everything good with your mom?" I asked. "Your sisters?"

"Yeah, they're all good. Bianca's son, Ethan, just started peewees. He's got some good stick work." Cruz sent me a look that let me know to drop the topic.

I gave him a faint nod. He'd tell me when he was ready… I hoped.

"If you don't want to talk to your parents, don't," Stol said. "They need to respect your wishes, but you should also be aware of theirs."

"I don't know if that's the best or worst advice ever," Maxim said. He gestured around. "Most of us didn't exactly have loving starts into the world."

Cruz's lips folded inward under the mass of his beard. "Do what you want, man, but remember, sometimes you don't get that second chance."

This was about the woman he'd mentioned when we flew out to San Jose. *Definitely* something going on with him. He lifted his shaggy head, met my gaze, and gave a tiny shake. *Not now*, his eyes pleaded. Oh, I was getting to the bottom of Cruz's issue. Most assuredly. But if he was that keen to keep it private, I'd respect his choice. For now.

"Good game," Coach said as he breezed in. "Naese, your statistics tonight are top of the league. Very impressive. Your parents are in the office. They said they need to speak to you."

My shoulders slumped. "Thanks, Coach."

His eyes swept over me. "You have twenty minutes to get cleaned up and talk before I'll need you for the presser."

I nodded, giving him a thankful glance. He moved over to our goalies, who had huddled with Adam, our former goalie turned coach.

With a heaviness I shouldn't feel after such a highlight reel of a game, I cleaned up. Then, feeling like each step brought me closer to doom, I headed toward the small guest coach's office. As I entered, my mother jumped out of her chair and hugged me with an exclamation of joy. I patted her back once before I let my hands fall. She stepped back, her expression hurt.

"I told you I didn't want to see you," I said to my father.

My mother gasped, her hands to her chest. "You don't mean that, Pax," she cried.

"I do. Thanks to your meddling, I lost the best part of my life. Hana was hurt, nearly died."

"And she doesn't want you back," my dad said with satisfaction as he leaned back in his chair.

I glared at him. "Is that why you're here? To fish for information?"

I looked over at my mother, whose eyes were wide with shock. Clearly, she hadn't been part of my father's scheme.

That was something. Maybe.

"You horrible, piece of…" I pulled in a breath as Dad straightened, his mouth slack and eyes burning. I pinned him with my glare. "Don't you dare involve yourself in my life. Ever. Again. As far as I'm concerned, you're dead to me."

My mother's pained cry barely registered as my father rose. "You'd do that—pick that, that girl over your family?" he asked.

"You ceased to be my family when you created a vendetta against the only woman I'll ever love. When you decided not to tell me Hana had been hurt, that Hana lost our baby, when you took away my choice to be there for her, to grieve with her. You took away my choices and pretended it was for my own good.

Except you didn't care that when you hurt her, you were hurting me, too. You knew that, and you *still* did this to us," I hissed.

"Pax—"

"No, Mom. I don't need a peacemaker. I need someone who actually cares about my feelings, my future."

"I do," Dad insisted. "That's why I want you to steer clear of the Sato girl."

I shook my head. "If you loved me, you'd want me to be happy. You'd want me to make my choices and live my life in the way that best suited me." I turned to my mother. I took her hand and squeezed her trembling fingers. "Goodbye."

I walked from the office with my head high.

"There are reasons you needed to break it off with her," Dad called after me. I kept walking. "She's not good for you, son."

"Is he really spouting *that* steaming pile?" Stolly asked as I joined him in the hallway. He took one look at my face, placed his hand on my shoulder, and squeezed. Then he moved forward into the office doorway. With a firm click, the door shut behind him, and Stol rained his riot act on my father's head.

The guys surrounded me as if I were a wounded member of the pack.

"Thanks," I said. "But I'm fine. Really."

"Thought you might want to see this," Maxim said. He started a video on his phone. Ida Jane, Millie, Keelie, Naomi, and Hana, all waved at the screen, yelling, "Go, Wildcatters!"

"She's at the watch party," Cormac said. He bumped my shoulder, offering the support I hadn't realized I needed.

"Ida Jane just sent this one, too," Maxim said. The next video popped up, and he handed me the phone.

"Tell me, truthfully now," Naomi coaxed. She sipped from her margarita glass. "What do you want?"

Ida Jane's video skills were crap; the camera tilted and shook enough to make me slightly seasick, but I couldn't look away.

Hana bit that lush pink lower lip as she stared at something I couldn't see. Her profile was lovely, all soft curves and delicate chin. Her thick, dark bangs were swept to the side, and I could make out the soft arch of her black eyebrow.

"I want to be happy. Fulfilled," she said, turning back toward Naomi. That gave me an excellent view of the sleek hair that fell in a fluid sheet down between her shoulder blades.

"How do you achieve that?" Naomi asked as she slurped her drink.

"I'm not sure."

"The NASA job?" Naomi prodded.

"That would go a long way…" Doubt filled Hana's voice.

"And?" Millie asked. I couldn't see her, but I knew her voice.

"And…" Hana heaved a sigh. "And I need to see what could be with Paxton."

The women cheered even more loudly than they had for our goal in the last video.

"The guys didn't score," Keelie said as the racket died down.

"Naese just did," Ida Jane said. "Probably the best one of his night."

"Keep in mind that if you stay with him, you'll be able to pay off your student loans faster," Millie said.

I hadn't thought about her loans. *I ought to do something about those*. Maybe that's how I could get her to agree to move in with me. I chewed the inside of my lip. That thought was manipulative, and I didn't want to manipulate Hana into staying with me…did I?

What if it's the only way I can get her to agree?

My stomach knotted as I worried over the right thing to do.

"Plus, he has the best house," Keelie said. "I'm in love with that walk-in closet."

"If you would have put more effort into the décor today…" Naomi said on a sigh.

"It's not my place to decorate Pax's house," Hana said.

"Um, yes, it is," Millie said. "He wants you to."

"I need to think about all this," Hana said.

The video ended.

I handed the phone back with shaking hands. "Send it to me?"

"Already did," Maxim assured me.

I nodded.

Coach called, "Need you, Naese."

I headed toward him.

"You should make another pass," Cormac said. "You know we don't always score the first time we shoot."

My lips twitched as I nodded again. "Get rid of my parents before Stolly rips off my dad's head."

"For what it's worth," Cruz said, falling into step next to me, "I think your father has an irrational fear of Hana."

"I know."

"And there's a reason for that," he said.

"Don't care."

Cruz grunted. He stopped at the door to the press conference. "Gotta feeling you will." He turned and headed back to the locker room.

~

After the press conference, we decided to grab a late dinner. We were all starving—common after a win—and we took over a great ramen place a few blocks from our hotel. The moment my bowl settled in front of me, I slurped the excellent pork broth from my large spoon and munched my mung beans and bamboo.

"Keelie really likes Hana," Cormac said next to me. He wielded his chopsticks like a pro, and I winced as my noodles slid back into my bowl.

"Millie, too." Stol scowled at his bowl of noodles and meat, having the same problem I was.

"That's because Hana's cool," Cruz said. He was even better with his chopsticks than Cormac, the big showoff. Somehow, he slurped the noodles without getting a drop of broth in his beard. That was just…inhuman. He pointed his chopsticks at me, which neatly held a perfect piece of meat between the little wooden ends. "She is cool."

"I know that. She's really funny, too. When she's not freaking out like she was with all the CATS today. Maybe that was a bad idea, having them with her there."

"They can be a little much," Cormac mused. "That's why we sent Paloma in. To diffuse. Plus, if Hana's going to be with you, she needs to know what she's getting into."

I slurped up noodly goodness. I loved this stuff—when I could get it in my mouth. "What's that?"

"We play hard and we love harder," Maxim said, leaning back in his chair.

That asshole had ordered bao…and used his hands. I wished I'd thought of that. I managed another bite, probably looking like the animated version of the Beast in the Disney film, so I went back to the spoon.

"That's right. Not only do we love hard, we do it as a family," Cormac said. "Which means we got your back, Naese."

"Thanks," I said.

"Slippery little shits," Stol said. He'd given up on the chopsticks and asked for a fork. He'd almost finished his big bowl while I was only about a quarter of the way through mine. "Your dad's a real piece of work, and I don't like him. Millie likes Hana, which means I will, too. Have her come over for dinner soon, yeah?"

"I'll try. But…" I grimaced and set down the chopsticks. "I can't make her stay with me. I need to offer to pay off her loans—"

"Whoa. Nope. No." Maxim shook his head.

"Not a good idea. She won't be receptive to that now," Cruz said. "You need to let her get used to the idea of being around you again. She's skittish because she was hurt, right? It's not going to be a quick transformation. She may fight you on this, but if you want her in your life, it'll be worth it."

"Then later, you don't offer to pay off the loans, you just do it." Maxim smirked. "And she'll be mad, say she wanted to be independent, but you'll tell her that's how you show her you love her."

"Can you believe he's happily married?" Cormac said with a long-suffering sigh.

"No accounting for taste," Stolly said cheerfully. "But Cruz is right. Show her how much she means to you. That worked for Millie and me." He grinned. "And I'm the dumb one of the group, so if I can pull it off, you totally can, Mr. Aeronautics."

"You're not dumb," Cruz said. "You have dyslexia. If that had been sorted when you were a kid, there were interventions that would make reading easier—"

"That's enough, big guy. I'm good," Stol said, patting Cruz's shoulder. "I'm fabulous."

Cruz studied him for a minute before nodding.

"Get her to stay with you," Cormac said. "Then you take the next step."

~

Once we made it back to the hotel, I lay in my bed and sent Hana a text.

Me: Once you move here, I'd really like you to stay with me. We deserve the chance to see if we still fit together.

I held my breath as the text went from delivered to read.

Three dots appeared…disappeared…*fuck*!…reappeared…*yes*! Answer me…

Hana: I'm thinking about it.

I blew out a breath.

Me: Anything I can do to help you make up your mind?

Hana: I don't think so. It's a mental thing. Fear's pretty difficult to overcome.

Me: Yeah, but it's not impossible. And we are a great team, Hana. The best. I know things ended badly, but think about before that. We were so good together, so happy.

I expected her to respond about the crash and the ensuing months when she struggled to survive. She surprised me instead.

Hana: If I do manage to overcome the initial fear hurdle, it may come back.

Me: And I'll prove to you each and every time that you made the right choice by giving us this second chance.

Hana: Okay.

I figured that was enough for tonight.

Me: Night, Hana.

Hana: I'll talk to you tomorrow. Great game, Pax.

I stared at the screen for a long moment.

Me: I love you.

I hit send and once again watched for the message to be read. Once I was sure she had, I closed my eyes and imagined how good it would feel to come home to Hana.

That was a dream—no, a *goal*—worth fighting tooth and nail for.

CHAPTER 18
Hana

"Well, here goes nothing," I mumbled. Once I had my seatbelt on, I clutched the steering wheel of Paxton's SUV—he'd had it shipped out to me so I had something to drive cross-country from San Jose to Houston. I'd gotten the job at NASA, and that was now my new home. The loon seemed to think I was capable of driving this beast after the two lessons he'd given me while I was in Houston last time.

"Crazy man," I said. But I smiled as I said it. He'd been patient, so like the Pax I remembered, and I'd struggled to pay attention to his instructions because I was busy watching his large hands on the wheel and the shift of light across the contours of his face.

His eyes changed color depending on the sunlight. I'd spent hours and hours studying his eyes while we were growing up. They were beautiful. Long lashed and under thick, nearly broody dark brows. His eyes were always focused on his task, and I'd liked it best when I was his task. Paxton had always made me feel like I was the center of his world when he turned that bright, determined expression toward me.

I shivered, missing it now. As he'd instructed, I depressed the brake and started the ignition. With exquisite care, once the SUV was in drive, I pulled away from the curb and eased into the narrow street. With a sigh of relief, I headed toward the traffic light, going five miles under the speed limit.

By the time I needed gas three hours later, I felt much more confident in my skills, and I turned on the radio, singing along as I sped along I-10. The scenery became less green as I hit the border with Arizona, and I marveled at the height of the saguaro cactus that dotted the landscape.

The last few weeks had been an absolute whirlwind. I was moving in with my ex-boyfriend after accepting the position at NASA. A small, petty part of me had wanted to yell, "*Take that, sucker!*" at Jeremy when I'd seen him in the coffee shop right after I'd signed my employment agreement, but his hangdog expression—coupled with his loss of Gunnar Evaldson's funding—had been more than enough recompense for his attempt at ruining my career.

Jeremy had caught my eye and made his way slowly over to me. He'd slid his hands into his chino pockets and rocked back on his heels. "I'm sorry for being such an ass," he'd told me.

The pinched expression on his face told me the apology had been tough to issue; therefore, I'd chosen magnanimity and nodded.

"*You're going to Houston?*" he'd asked.

Ours was a small industry of terrible gossips; he'd known the answer to that question long before I nodded again. His expression had fallen further, as had his shoulders.

"*Good luck. It's an incredible opportunity.*"

"*Thanks,*" I'd said.

He'd swallowed and grimaced. "*You're getting back with the athlete, aren't you?*"

I'd shrugged. "*We're friendly again. I've missed him in my life.*" I'd leaned in closer. "*And just so you know, Paxton studied astrophysics. He recently graduated from Rice University—top of his class. And he was the one to get me interested into the field back in high school.*"

I didn't mention that he'd piqued my interest when we were nine, and he'd built a rocket out of leftover corrugated metal that we'd played in for the next three years. Paxton told the story differently—saying I'd been the reason for *his* interest in space. I guess who'd captivated whom didn't matter as much as that we'd both focused on a similar degree.

Jeremy's eyes had widened. "*Guess I was wrong on all counts,*" he'd mumbled.

When he'd turned on his heel and walked away, I hadn't bothered to watch him go. I'd just snapped the plastic lid onto my to-go coffee and smiled as I'd headed out into the watery sunshine, happy to be boxing up my meager belongings and excited to see Paxton.

By the second day of the drive, I was stiff from all the sitting, so I took some time to poke through Old Town Albuquerque during an early lunch, enjoying the warm air and the backdrop of Sandia Mountain as I nibbled on green-chile-slathered enchiladas.

"Too bad New Mexico doesn't have a professional hockey team," I murmured.

The older gentleman seated at the counter next to me chuckled. "Hija, we don't have any professional teams. Our whole state population is smaller than most major cities." He smiled kindly and tipped his head toward the mountain I'd been admiring. "But we got something nicer, no?"

I smiled back, relaxed and lighter now that I was nearly a thousand miles from Jeremy and Space Elevated. "You do. Got any work in the aerospace industry?"

"You haven't heard of the Space Port? You don't know about the NASA contract with UNM?" He clucked his tongue. "Definitely not a local." Again, he smiled. "Let's just keep that industry between you and me, 'kay?"

He chuckled as he took a bite of his beans, and I nodded. But I was intrigued. It was pretty here. I'd have to find out more about the NASA connections.

I spent that night in a small Texas town that had three motels to choose from, along with two gas stations and a truck stop. My bed was clean, but the food wasn't as good as the Albuquerque restaurant, so I hustled back on the road in the morning.

Six hours later, I made it to Houston. Or, as Paxton called it, *driving hell.* After living in a small New England hamlet and then in the tightly packed housing of the Bay Area, I remained unprepared for driving through the Houston sprawl. The edges of the city began with the typical gas stations and truck stops, but those went on and on, interspersed with farmland and strip malls, for miles—until I hit the suburbs with their amalgam of houses and shops and restaurants.

I gasped, feeling growing trepidation as a car slid across the multiple lanes of traffic, missing my bumper by mere inches.

"Oh my…"

Nope, I wasn't used to this. Culture shock set in harder when I made out the dual downtowns: the first was larger and filled with high-rises that had to be one hundred stories. The second set of skyscrapers was slightly south and west. That, I knew, was the Galleria and the general area of Paxton's home—the place I would be staying until I figured out what to do about lodging. Despite Paxton's relentless welcome, I told myself I could still find my own place, if I needed to for any reason.

But it was time to move forward. Was all this serendipity? Had fate decided Paxton and I were meant to be together, or was I reading too much into this newest round of upheaval? Right now, there was no way to know. The only certitude I had was that Houston drivers were aggressive, and this city was actually an amalgam of former townships that had been swallowed in its constant growth.

It took another harrowing forty-five minutes, but I finally pulled into Paxton's driveway. I cut the engine and closed my eyes, needing a moment to calm down. But then excited chatter heading toward me had me lifting my head.

Ida Jane led the pack, coming toward me confidently with a big wave and bigger smile. Behind her were the four other women I recognized, three of whom had babies strapped to them in various fabric contraptions. The fourth was older by about a decade, with flame-colored hair and the sleekest pair of green glasses I'd ever seen. Paloma, the coach's wife. She exuded a friendly capability I wanted to achieve.

New life goal added to my list right there.

"You're here!" Ida Jane said as she opened my door. "I brought the welcoming crew."

Millie, Keelie, and Naomi, all of whom kept contact with some part of their babies, be it tiny head or bottom, smiled at me and waved.

"They're sleeping," Keelie said in a hushed voice. "So we don't want to jiggle them too much with hugs. But later, we'll squeeze you hard to show you how happy we are that you're here!"

I grinned back, excited to spend more time with this great group. "I'll look forward to the dog pile."

Naomi snorted. "Girl, don't give me ideas."

Paloma offered a bright smile. "Let's get you out of the car and give those legs a good stretch. Houston traffic is a nightmare no matter the time of day, but any time after about two o'clock and you're in for it."

I nodded. My leg throbbed from being still too long, and I wobbled as I stood. Nothing new there, but I hated the pins-and-needles sensation that followed. The women waited patiently, not commenting on my issue, for which I was very thankful.

"Are drivers here always so…"

"Aggressive? Annoying?" Millie asked.

"With a death wish?" Naomi asked. She nodded. "Yes."

"I'd say you get used to it, and I guess you do, sort of." Ida Jane wrinkled her nose. "But it's still shocking when someone tries to rip off your back bumper at seventy miles per hour. I don't like to drive."

"Which is why you make Uber or Maxim take you everywhere," Millie added.

"Not true!" Ida Jane shot back. "I make you drive, too."

They smiled at each other, and I could see the years of friendship connecting them.

"Well, let's see what you've got, what you need, and what you think of the transformation to the house," Naomi said.

"And then we'll watch the game," Paloma said.

"But not properly because most of us can't have alcohol," Naomi said on a sigh.

"I brought some of those mocktail drinkie-things," Millie said.

"Yay," Keelie exclaimed. "I call a fake G and T!"

My head bounced around as I tried to process it all. I once again envied these women their strong bond. Would I ever be part of it? I was quiet, preferring to observe rather than dive in, but I should have realized they wouldn't let me hang on the sidelines exclusively.

"Don't mind them," Paloma said kindly. She touched my shoulder, letting me know she was a hugger.

Good. I wanted one of those—*many* of those—in my life. After spending most of my years deprived of human touch, I was like parched ground to mist. I soaked it up and wished for more. I'd missed Paxton's easy touch more than just about anything. With him, I'd felt seen, wanted, loved. Since he'd left me, I'd struggled to connect.

"They're exuberant," I said.

"We are." Naomi winked. "Our joie de vivre is half of our charm."

"What's the other half?" Millie wanted to know. She shoved her thick, dark frames up her button nose. She was cute in the way many of the women I worked with were: great bone structure and features, long lashes, and a seeming disregard for makeup or even matching clothes.

With Millie, I'd felt an immediate connection. She'd understand my stress about a specific, difficult assignment or research in a way that sensuous and confident Naomi wouldn't. I wasn't yet sure about Keelie, who seemed observant and quieter than Ida Jane or Naomi.

"All right. Let's all grab something from the tailgate and bring it in to Hana's room," Paloma said, taking charge.

I had a feeling that was often her role. I clicked open the locks and stood to the side as the women chattered, each grabbing a bag or box from the trunk. Their babies all cuddled in close.

"How did they synchronize the kids' nap schedules?" I asked Paloma.

She smiled. "They didn't. But babies tend to sleep better and deeper when connected to their mother."

"Ah." Not my most brilliant response, but the only one that came to mind.

Paloma grabbed a bigger box, so I did the same. "Naese said you have a brother."

"Yes, Aiki." I bit my lip. "He's a year older than Paxton. We're not that close."

We hadn't been since he'd broken down and admitted he was jealous of Paxton and had poisoned Mother against him. I hadn't figured out how—or if—I could forgive him.

"Because of Naese?" Paloma asked. She seemed to already know the answer.

"In part. Aiki was a great athlete, but not as good as Pax."

Paloma hummed. "Few are. You aren't the first person to tell me that's caused discord." She shook her head. "These guys seem like they have it all—and they have an awful lot, don't get me wrong—but it's not as wonderful or easy as outsiders think. Constant jealousy, performance anxiety, the threat of trades and demotions. It can be emotionally as well as physically taxing. That's why we work so hard to foster relationships between the players and with the CATS. A strong support system makes a huge difference for the players' and their families' quality of life."

"Ending up with the Houston organization saved Cormac," Keelie said, returning for another box. "He was well on his way to derailment without Silas's mentorship."

"I'll be sure to tell Silas you said so," Paloma said. She sat her box in the entry hall, and I bent down to do the same.

As I rose, I gasped. "What…" I couldn't push any more words past my lips—too overwhelmed by Pax's house. It was *perfect.* "You…"

"Paxton gave us the scrapbook," Millie said as she surveyed the space.

"Since you were hesitant to spend your man's money when you were here before, we decided to help out with the first step, so you'd be comfortable living here," Naomi said.

"Naomi's great at finding bargains—and beautiful things," Ida Jane said with a hint of rancor and a lot of admiration.

"You're getting there, little grasshopper," Naomi countered.

They all laughed. I was still dazed by the transformation.

The house no longer looked like a single man's bachelor pad. It looked just like the house I'd planned for us during that last year we were together.

These women and Paxton had recreated my dream home.

"Oh," I gasped. Tears sprung to my eyes.

I'd spent hours cutting out pictures and taping them into my dreams book. I'd wanted to create what I'd never had: a home. Paxton's house now had the double crown molding, the shiplap, even the reclaimed wood floors I'd sighed and dreamed over.

I swallowed the lump of emotion building in my throat as I moved to the kitchen. It was the same as when I'd left last month. I took comfort in the glossy, black French stove and hood, all done up in brass. The white cabinets and countertops were spotless, but they warmed me deeply.

"This is…amazing," I whispered as I turned back to the living room. They'd matched the exact shade of red I'd wanted for the large sectional and loveseat that cozied around a geometric-patterned rug and a low, live-edged cube of wood that had to be two and a half feet across.

"We know it's not *exactly* what you had in the book," Ida Jane said.

"I figured you'd want vegan leather, especially since it was the only place we could get the sectional and loveseat made up in time," Millie said.

"Y-yes. Vegan? Really? That's cool." I smiled.

"The cube coffee table was all Paxton. He saw it and said it was very Hana," Keelie added, her tone earnest.

These women were nervous. Of my reaction. Even Naomi

shuffled her feet—Naomi, the queen of confidence.

"I love it. I—I'm overwhelmed…"

"Don't show her the bedroom yet," Ida Jane said from the corner of her mouth, her eyes dancing.

"You decorated the guest room?" I asked.

"Well, sure, but that's for Paxton." Naomi decreed as if it was normal to kick the home's owner out of the primary suite and into a guest one.

I shook my head. Paloma settled her hand on my shoulder. "Paxton wants you in the big bedroom. He said it has a better bathtub for your leg, and he said it was better for you take the stairs as it would help rebuild the muscles around the injury."

I gulped. "That sneaky—" My chest heaved.

"Oh! We pushed too hard," Millie moaned.

"We just want you to be happy," Keelie fretted.

"Are you okay?" Paloma asked quietly.

"Yes." My voice came out strong and steady. "I am."

And I was. Because with these alterations to his home and lifestyle, Paxton was showing me he wanted me here. He'd made sure his friends' wives were here to greet me, even though I'd also texted the CATS to let them know my plans. Some of my fear that he was using me to assuage his guilt melted away much like a chunk of rock eroding under the pressure of a stream.

He loved me. He'd told me so. Now he was showing me. I just had to believe.

I smiled at the women. "I think I need to see this amazing bedroom."

"I'll bring up your suitcase," Paloma said.

"Then we'll have some tea and cookies," Ida Jane said.

"She makes the best cookies," Millie said. "Beware of them. They're addicting."

"No way Hana will get to eat that many if Paxton's around," Keelie said. "Cormac inhales them, leaving me crumbs." She shot a glance at the door where Paloma had just gone. "Oof, I probably shouldn't have said that."

"No worries." Naomi waved her hand. "Adam was a constant diet cheater, and he did just fine." She glanced over at me, her expression filled with pride. "Sixteen years in the league."

"That is impressive," I murmured.

"Naese should have as many," Paloma said as she returned. "Well, as long as he stays healthy."

"That's the kicker, isn't it?" Keelie said on a sigh. "But Adam did, and so has Cruz. I guess we just keep expecting the good—"

"Even as we prepare for something unexpected," Millie said with a nod.

That's what I was doing with Paxton: soaking up the good right now. Still, I should prepare my escape route for when this glorious, almost-too-perfect time in my life ended. It always ended—my father's death, my mother and brother's disdain, Paxton leaving me, the accident. Every time I thought life was wonderful, it imploded. So, I should look soon to find my own place to live and not rely on Paxton. *Why had I agreed to stay with him in the first place?*

Well, actually I knew. Paxton had asked nicely, and I'd wanted to agree. But that didn't make staying here smart. So why did it feel wrong to consider leaving now that I stood looking at everything he'd done for me? I took a deep breath, determined to slow my whirling brain.

~

After my emotional arrival, the women and I managed to get my things unpacked and put away in Paxton's former bedroom. I tried to kick up a fuss about that, but those five women were forces of nature, and I realized quickly that I didn't stand a chance of winning. I didn't have much, so I figured I could move out of the beautifully appointed bedroom after they left.

Dragging my hand across the cranberry silk duvet, I sighed, already missing the chance to sleep in the beautiful bed with its mountain of pillows. The rest of the room wasn't that different from the last time I'd been here, but Paxton had hung up a series of black and white photos of the two of us. They took up an entire wall—a feat considering the room had such high ceilings. The photos started when we were in elementary school. The cascade downward showcased us together at various events from campouts in Paxton's yard to his hockey games to school dances and prom, and then our college years when we'd been apple picking and skiing.

The montage stole my breath and made my fingers shake as I touched one of the frames. It was my favorite: the image of Paxton and me bundled up after a day on the slopes. I smiled at the camera, rosy-cheeked, and he looked at me with so much love and pride.

"Damn, girl." Keelie whistled. "That's one scorching look."

"Know where that led," Naomi said as she walked past, patting her waking baby's bottom as she moved toward the cavernous closet where Paloma was busy hanging up my work clothes.

I looked away. It had led to a hot night of tangled sheets, sweat, moans, and a whole lot of pleasure.

I hadn't let myself think about that particular part of our relationship for years; losing Paxton had been too painful to even consider revisiting the good times. And that night had been the *best*, especially when he'd brushed my hair back from my damp forehead and stared deep into my eyes.

"*You're my future,*" he'd said.

"*You're my life,*" I'd replied as I rested my cheek against him.

"*I love you, Hana. So much.*"

I'd fallen asleep with his words in my ear, our skin still connected.

Mere months later, he'd broken my heart.

"His dad showed up at a game recently," Ida Jane said. She studied the pictures.

I turned toward her, but she remained in profile. She reached out and straightened the edge of a frame.

"And?"

Finally, Ida Jane turned toward me. "From what I heard, his dad warned him away from you—"

"And Luka stepped in and chewed that horrible man's butt to paste—" Millie began.

"After Naese disowned his parents," Paloma said. She'd stepped out of the closet, holding one of my blouses on a hanger. "I like this. Where'd you get it?"

"Vintage consignment shop in San Francisco," I answered.

"Pax disowned his parents?" I shook my head. "I don't want to cause strife between them."

"You didn't," Keelie called from the bathroom. She poked her head out. "Finished putting away your toiletries, and don't even think about moving out of that gorgeous bathroom or I'll pinch you. Hard." She narrowed her eyes.

"Those people and their choices created this situation," Naomi said. "They're reaping what they sowed. Don't worry about them or Naese. We've made sure he's taken care of." She had a no-nonsense tone that made me wonder what else she'd taken care of.

As I group, we trooped back down the stairs, and I settled between Millie and Keelie as Paloma and Ida Jane whipped up some appetizers to go with the tea and cookies. Evidently we needed fuel to watch the game.

"Don't worry, we won't use the stove. That first time is for you and Naese," Ida Jane said.

My flush made Naomi and Keelie giggle, but Millie was off on the other side of the room, changing her daughter's diaper. Bree, I'd learned, was the oldest of the babies at seven months. Brooks, Keelie's son, was five months, and Naomi's son, Felix, was just past his three-month birthday.

"How'd you manage the timing for that?" I asked.

Naomi snorted. "Copious amounts of sex." Millie returned in time to fist-bump her. My eyes widened.

Paloma settled a platter or cheese and fruit on the coffee table. "Ignore them, especially Naomi. She's back in the honeymoon phase post-baby."

"How do you turn on Naese's TV? I swear, these guys have more remotes than NASA," Keelie griped.

I giggled. "No, they don't. But I wouldn't be surprised if Paxton tried. He wanted to be an aerospace engineer."

All of the women turned to focus on me. "Well, I didn't expect that," Naomi murmured.

"Do tell," Millie said. "I adore the thought of Naese with a pocket protector."

"Oh my gosh." Naomi gasped. "He would be the hottest guy in that room." She waved a hand in front of her face.

I couldn't help but giggle again.

"Here, you do it," Keelie said, exasperated. She dropped five remotes in my lap. After studying them for a few moments, I managed to turn on the TV and get it to the right channel for the game.

"Apparently it takes a NASA scientist to turn on the jerk's television," Millie said. She winked to let me know she was joking.

"Now, spill the goods," Ida Jane said. She popped a grape in her mouth and looked at me expectantly.

"What do you want to know?"

Millie leaned forward. "*Everything*."

"I already told you—"

"About the breakup," Naomi said, leaning forward. "But we want to know all the goods on Naese."

The other women nodded.

So, I started talking.

CHAPTER 19

Hana

"The guys scored," Paloma said after I'd finished telling them about growing up down the street from Paxton, my brother's struggles, and my mom's vindictive control, all of which had contributed to Paxton's eventual decision to break up with me.

After a brief hesitation, I added the details about my miscarriage and Paxton not responding to the texts I'd sent him until he showed up in California.

Millie sat, a piece of popcorn almost to her lips, just staring.

Ida Jane growled. "I'm going to throttle him."

"I could whack him with my putter," Keelie offered.

"Oh! They scored twice," Naomi said, glancing over at the game. "And you didn't have his number anymore. You told us that, Hana. His father changed it, remember?"

Paloma rose from her wingback chair and headed into the kitchen. She came back with the pitcher of virgin mojitos Naomi had mixed and topped off our glasses. "Silas didn't sign him out of the draft because of his behavior after he broke up with you," she noted. "He said Naese was less grounded, wilder, than he'd originally thought. If Lewis had worked out instead of choking for the first forty games, I'm not sure Silas would have ever considered Naese again." She squeezed my hand gently. "I just thought you should know that."

"Well, I can't say I want bad things for Pax," I told them. "He was my safe harbor for years."

"Until he betrayed you," Ida Jane said.

"Led around by his dick." Naomi shook her head.

"Some of them do go wild," Millie said.

A look of understanding passed between Ida Jane, Millie, and Naomi—one I didn't totally comprehend. But I realized we were part of the same sisterhood. We'd gotten involved with men who had much more extensive sexual histories than we did.

"I don't like how that makes me feel," I said. I wrapped my hands around my elbows.

"None of us do," Naomi said quietly.

"I'm not sure it's a good idea to be here now, but I couldn't stay in that lab with Jeremy, not after what Jeremy did," I said. "He manipulated me. And no man should grab and threaten a woman—or anyone."

"You got that right," Millie said. "If you ever want to learn self-defense, I've been thinking about teaching a class."

"Ooooh, I'd like that for Trix and me," Paloma said. "Beatrix is our daughter," she explained to me.

"Cool. Now that I've decided not to return to my position, I'm looking for something to do," Millie said.

"Besides blow millions of bucks?" Ida Jane said. She bumped shoulders with her friend.

Millie sighed. "Yes, Idge, besides that."

Keelie wrapped a supportive arm around my shoulders. "If it doesn't work out with Naese, just tell one of us. We'll help you get on your feet. You shouldn't have to stay trapped in a situation where you aren't happy simply because it's what's available. And for the record, I've always found Naese to be far more even-keel than some of these boneheads. No disrespect." She offered a smile to the group.

"You can throw Silas into the group of boneheads in his youth," Paloma noted. "It's part of why he was disappointed in Naese and didn't draft him like he'd originally planned. It's not that he doesn't believe in second chances—"

"Silas is *great* about second chances," Keelie piped in.

"And our guys managed to get past their mistakes and make solid decisions for their current circumstances and their futures," Ida Jane said. "I mean, by the time I met Maxim, he was years past sowing wild oats."

"Same with Adam," Naomi added.

"And Silas," Paloma said. "And Naese."

"It doesn't make your stomach knot to know they've had those experiences with other women?" I asked.

"Every damn time I thought about it, for years," Naomi said. "Which was too often." She took a sip of her drink and set it aside with a sigh. She smiled at her son playing with his toes on the thick, soft blanket at her feet. "But there came a point that I had to decide: was I going to focus on a past I couldn't change or create a life and a future I wanted—that I controlled?"

She grimaced. "I *detest* Adam's past. He knows that. He works hard to ensure I know I'm his priority now. Well, me and this little guy. But I had to choose to forgive him for things he did before I knew him."

I licked my lips. "That's the difference. I was with Paxton, and he left me—alone—so he could party and hook up."

"But now you know it was his father's urging," Keelie said.

"And your mother, too, from what Paxton and your brother told you," Ida Jane added. "I mean, that's a lot of pressure."

I stared down at my hands in my lap. "If he loved me enough, wouldn't he have fought for me—for us?"

"Sounds like a question you'll need to ask him," Paloma said. "And while I'm not defending his choice, he was young. Young people often listen to their parents."

"As good a job as you've done talking through the original sticking point and breakup, there still seem to be things you two need to work out," Ida Jane said.

"I get the sense there's more to the story than possibly even Naese knows," Paloma said, watching me carefully.

I'd wondered the same thing. It just seemed odd that once Paxton and I had gotten serious, like *marriage* serious, his dad had started pushing for us to break up. I knew Mr. Naese and my mother didn't get along, but that shouldn't have had any bearing on my relationship with Paxton. I worried my lower lip.

"I think you need to know what that is so you can decide whether or not you can forgive Naese for his choice," Millie said.

"And if I can't?" I looked over at Ida Jane. "That's why I left after the game. There doesn't seem to be a point to building a relationship with you all—as wonderful as you've been—if I'm going to lose you."

"That's not how the CATS work," Paloma said. "We're a tight-knit group. A *family*. And we still support our CATS, even if they divorce or break up."

"It can get awkward if the new partner shows up at the same event as a former partner, but I don't think we've had any serious issues," Keelie said, glancing around to confirm. The others nodded.

"I'm the quiet one," I said. "I don't make friends that quickly or easily."

"Neither do most of us, contrary to how we may seem," Naomi said. "A lot of us have our own trauma, our own reasons not to trust easily. I think that's a big part of why we can be so welcoming."

Brooks started to cry, which set off Bree. Both Keelie and Millie moved away to deal with their babies.

When they all headed out, with apologies, a few minutes later, all I could do was exhale in relief. Paloma caught me doing so and smiled. "We're a lot, I know, but our hearts are good."

"They are," I agreed.

She gave me a friendly side hug and then she, too, was gone.

I stared around the large, empty house and sighed. "Well, time to clean up."

By the time I'd put everything away, I was too tired to climb the stairs. I settled on the couch and tucked myself in.

"I'll move my stuff to the guest room tomorrow," I mumbled as I closed my eyes.

I have no idea how long I'd been out when a set of warm arms slid around me, cuddling me to thick pectoral muscle. "Pax," I mumbled, snuggling closer to his familiar smell and solid bulk.

"Right here, baby."

He carried me up the stairs and helped me into bed. He

smoothed my hair from my face. I lifted one droopy eyelid and offered him a smile. Pax grinned back. He knelt next to the bed with a soft, happy expression. "Ah, Hana, I'm glad you're here, in my house, in this bed, where you belong."

I bit my lip because in that moment, I wanted nothing more than to belong to him. I clasped his wrist as he lifted his hand from my temple. "Stay with me?"

His smile turned dazzling. "Nothing I want more."

I buried into the pillows, lulled into slumber by the softness. He slid in behind me and his arm wrapped around my middle, his nose buried in my hair.

"I love you, Hana," he said. His voice cracked. "I've missed you *terribly.*"

And for the first time, I truly believed him.

CHAPTER 20
Paxton

Holding Hana in my arms again was a dream come true. She was warm and soft and smelled delicious—like Hana. I slid into a deep, welcome rest and woke more refreshed than I'd been in months, possibly years…and with a raging hard-on nestled between Hana's slender thighs. I yawned as I snuggled my hips closer. Hana whimpered, pressing her cute butt against my groin.

Awake now, I rocked forward again, groaning at how good the friction felt against my dick. Much to my surprise, Hana wiggled her ass and arched even closer.

"You feel good," I murmured.

"More, Paxton." She panted as she pressed back. "I need more!"

I smiled, enjoying her demanding tone. I tightened my arm across her waist and splayed my fingers over her belly as I rocked against her. She whimpered my name. I ground into her soft ass and thighs again and again.

Our breathing quickened, and sweat bloomed along her neck. I nuzzled into her warm skin and licked the saltiness as I rocked back and forth. "Han…not going to last… You're so special to me, baby…so sweet."

"T-touch me," Hana begged. "I need to come. Gah—I need to come!" Her soft voice shrilled as she thrust her hips back against me. I shifted my hips so I could bump against her soft, sweet little ass. We panted as we ground together, our limbs and breaths intertwined.

She keened as she stiffened, her body wound tight, like she might break. And she did… I picked up the pace as her juices soaked her panties and my briefs. Delicious tension built at the base of my spine, my balls drew up tight…and I crested, too.

The release went on and on, thick and rich, draining in the best possible way. It was only after a moment, when my breathing began to even out, that I realized Hana had removed my hand from her knee.

I sat up. "Did I hurt you?" I asked, horror seeping through the relaxation and euphoria.

She shook her head but kept her chin tilted to her chest. "No. I should shower."

"Hana…"

"It's fine, Pax. Really." She smiled over her shoulder, but it didn't reach her normally warm brown eyes. "It was really, really good. Thank you."

She scooted off the bed and wobbled toward the bathroom. I looked at my saturated underwear and flopped onto my back with a curse. I glanced over at the closed bathroom door and finally understood how the women I'd slept with during that first year Hana and I were apart must have felt. I'd thanked them for getting me off, then I'd jetted out of their lives.

"Rejection fucking sucks," I muttered.

It was even worse from the person I loved, but I should have known Hana wasn't ready for intimacy.

Before, we'd shared *everything*. Been each other's first and learned to love together. Now, we'd had our own lives, lovers, and disappointments that didn't include the other person. Relearning and realigning together wasn't as easy as one amazingly good orgasm. Unfortunately.

And I'd need to be vulnerable, put myself out there, if I wanted to reconnect to Hana. She'd been brave enough to come here, to give me this chance. I wasn't going to mess it up.

So if she needed a bit of space to regroup, I'd give it to her, but that didn't mean I'd let her hide from our chemistry, from how good we'd been together. She and I both deserved this chance to explore each other's bodies and hearts. We also deserved that happy-ever-after so many of my teammates were living.

As I stared at the ceiling, I vowed to get there with her. Whatever it took. I was all in.

Hana

I pulled in a breath as I stared at my flushed face in the mirror. "You dry-humped Paxton to the best orgasm you've had in years."

My lips twisted because the only others that compared to the tingling deliciousness still sizzling through my body right now were the climaxes Paxton had given me years ago. He'd learned to play my body to perfection—or maybe my body had wanted him to play it to perfection and capitulated easily. Whatever the reason, I was still giddy from the high-school-style sex session.

"We shouldn't have done that," I muttered. "We can't do that again."

I gave myself a nod, even though I wasn't sure why I was acting this way. I yearned to crawl back into bed with Pax and rub against him everywhere until he made me come and come and come until I passed out.

Yet that seemed irresponsible. Hedonistic…*perfect.*

No! Right the urge and get in the shower. Get clean and gain perspective.

"Staying here was a mistake," I said.

"It's not a mistake," Paxton called through the door. "*We're* not a mistake. What happened in our bed wasn't a mistake. And I'm glad you're here. Don't make it weird, Han."

I couldn't help but smile, even as I rolled my eyes. "Don't make it weird," I whispered.

Everything was weird.

And I was happy, most probably because of the weirdness.

After my shower and a fresh set of clothes over my brace, I squared my shoulders and headed into the empty bedroom. I blinked. Where was Paxton? Didn't he want to talk? We should talk.

My nose twitched at the scent of coffee. I headed down the stairs, holding the banister for support. Paxton was in the kitchen, his damp hair curling at his neck and ears. He wore track pants and a dark T-shirt that had been washed one too many times to call it black.

"Hey," he said cautiously. He raised his mug and took a sip, seemingly so he didn't say anything else. After setting it down, he picked up another thick, ceramic mug and offered it to me. The tea tag fluttered, and I noted that it was a brand of breakfast tea I'd preferred when I was in college.

Warmth saturated my chest as I realized how hard he was

trying. Still, my steps were hesitant as I eased toward him, accepting the offering. Our fingers brushed, and his pupils dilated as I took a breath.

The air between us seemed to crackle as we stared at each other. Eventually his face softened, and he stepped back, leaving me bereft and thankful—two mutually exclusive options that were somehow deeply connected. Emotions were hard to grapple with, but I needed to do so.

"So…" I began. I took a fortifying sip of tea, wincing slightly at the heat on my palate. "So…I don't regret what we did."

Paxton's chest expanded and his Adam's apple dipped. "Good." His voice was rough, a bit scratchy with emotion. "Good. I don't either."

"We still have incredible chemistry."

Paxton nodded as he lowered his mug. A drop of coffee settled in the dip between the two halves of his lower lip, and I fantasized about leaning up to lick it off. Instead, I sipped from my mug.

"But we're going at a breakneck speed, and you want to take things slower," he said. "Be more measured, right?"

I stared at Paxton, and my heart cried out that *no*, I should shove him against the wall and ravish him. I yearned to feel him inside me, surrounding me, loving and cherishing me.

But that wasn't smart. That was falling back into the previous pattern that had left me in a hospital bed in tears. It was my turn to heave a deep, cleansing breath. "I don't blame you for my accident," I said, because it needed saying. He wasn't responsible, and I should alleviate any guilt he felt. "Aiki drove that car into the other driver. Aiki insisted on coming with my mother. Aiki is the reason my leg's never going to be the same."

That needed to be said, too.

Paxton settled his hips against the counter behind him, seeming to wait patiently for me to finish my thought and work through my emotions.

"So, yeah. That's *that* part of our current situation—the past we needed to work through. And I have to say, jumping back into an intimate relationship with you would be satisfying," I told him.

Paxton's lips quirked in that partial grin I loved so much.

"But it would also mean I've fully accepted and forgiven you," I continued. "That I'm ready to move forward." I cleared my throat and forced myself to meet Paxton's sad eyes. "I'm not there yet."

His lush lips compressed. "I get that. I *respect* that. Which is why I suggested you come here, stay with me—get to know me again. I'm not going to pressure you, Hana. It's too important for us to be together. I won't push you for even some delicious sex before you're ready. I don't want you to have doubts you can't overcome. I'll be here for you, and for now, that's as a friend. Just know that I want more. Much more than that." He paused a moment, and then laid his last cards on the table. "I want forever. For us to be a family, whatever form that takes. Kids, no kids, fur kids...whatever we decide works for us. That's what I want, with you."

I nodded because my throat was too tight for words.

"I need more than that, Hana," he said after a moment.

I took another sip of my tea and cleared my throat. "I'm pretty sure I want that, too, with you. I just need—I need time, Pax. To trust in this, in loving you, again."

"Can you say it?" he asked hesitantly. He swallowed, his Adam's apple dipping low. "Please."

I knew what he needed, because I'd needed the words as well as the actions. I needed it all, and I should have known he did, too. "I love you, Paxton."

He closed his eyes and every muscle in his face, then in his shoulders, relaxed. "I love you, too."

Before I figured out what to say, Paxton's stomach rumbled loudly. He placed a hand against it and grimaced. "Any chance I can talk you into firing up this insane contraption so we can eat something?"

I set my mug aside with a smile. "If you're sure…"

"It was for you, Han. Of course I'm sure."

Delight danced across my skin. "Yeah, I'd love to whip up something. What do you want? Eggs? An omelet? Pancakes?"

"Yes," Paxton moaned, clutching his abdomen. I noted the faint ridges of muscle as the shirt settled there. He was built for explosive speed and precision, pretty much the opposite of me.

That was okay. I was small next to his large frame. I was quieter next to his voice for opinions and feelings. I was cautious while he was more than willing to jump quickly into something he cared about.

We were opposites in many ways, except when it came to each other. In that, we'd always been in sync. And after a few minutes, we once again fell into an easy rhythm of Paxton cutting and chopping and mixing while I ordered him around.

We made omelets with avocado, spinach, tomato, and bacon and then a thick stack of whole-wheat power pancakes held together with bananas, topped with sliced strawberries and blueberries.

While we worked, we discussed Paxton's upcoming game schedule and my new position, which I'd start on Monday. It was companionable—*nice*. It was everything I'd missed and yearned for the past few years.

After Paxton had demolished the majority of both dishes and proclaimed the expensive range more than worth it, he sat back in his chair and stared at me over the rim of his second and last cup of coffee. "Would you be willing to come to our game on Tuesday? I know you're just starting your job and it may be a lot, but you can sit in the owner's box with Gunnar—I asked him, and he's delighted to host you. There's plenty of food, and you'll have more room to stretch your leg than if you're down in the stands. I can drive you home afterward, if you want to wait for me."

Instead of answering his question, I asked, "How are you going to get around if I have your car?"

"Well, I have another vehicle. But more than likely I'll have one of the guys swing by and pick me up. There's a reason we're all in this neighborhood."

I smiled at him as I set my knife and fork at the edge of my plate, aligned just so, as my mother had always insisted. She'd been a stickler for proper etiquette. It was a habit I'd chosen to maintain after her death.

Most of her habits I hadn't liked—including the berating and belittling she often did of me and Aiki. It was no wonder my brother had turned to substances. Living with a person who never saw you as good enough, never praised you or said they loved you—that messed with self-confidence and the ability to be open to new relationships.

I still had some stuff to work out and through.

"I'd love to come to your game," I told him, pushing my concerns away. Paxton hadn't asked me to do something I didn't want to do. Supporting him and his work was important, and he'd shown a great capacity for cheering me on; I could and would offer him the same. "Let's plan on that. But I might be a little late. I really want to learn the applications the team's using so I can be up to speed and helpful when they do the next simulation."

Paxton nodded. "Of course. That's in late March, right?"

I smiled because he was just as interested in the work I was doing as I was. "Yes. Dr. Gerenstein said we'll test some of my theory on the alloys to keep them from getting too cold and brittle in space. Up to now, it's all been theoretical because I haven't had access to the practical application."

"Even with Space Elevated?"

"Nope. We had simulations, but nothing as state of the art as the zero-gravity lab here."

"You're great at math, so I'm sure you nailed it," Paxton said. He glanced at the clock. I raised my eyebrows.

"We were invited over to Cormac and Keelie's for a barbecue. That is, if you're interested…"

My smile widened. "Oh yeah, let's go. After I clean this up—"

"I'll clean up," Paxton said firmly. "You made the food—"

"You helped!"

"And I enjoyed eating it. Now you can get ready or relax,

whatever you want, while I clean up in here. Then we'll head on over, okay?"

~

And that's how we spent the next couple of weeks: enjoying each other's company, me attending Paxton's home games and discussing my work with him on the late-night rides home. We no longer slept together because Paxton respected my need for time and space, and I restrained from inviting him in. I missed him in the bed, but the time to get to know each other was invaluable.

Whenever Paxton was within reach, I found myself touching him Typically, it was just being close, but he liked to hold hands or sling his arm over my shoulders. I loved placing my palm on his thick, hard thigh when we sat on the couch.

It was a slow dance of reconnecting and letting the thrum of desire reach a fever pitch between us. I loved every second of our intricate maneuvering. The euphoria of falling in love with Paxton all over again spilled into my work, letting me connect more easily with my new teammates.

Everything was going well, yet I couldn't help that niggle of doubt that kept slithering into my consciousness. It kept asking me if I deserved to be this happy when it had been my choice to leave school that day that had inadvertently caused my mother's death.

CHAPTER 21
Hana

I stared at the Wildcatters hockey game on the TV screen, unseeing. The CATS and I sat in Paxton's living room—my house, too, as I'd been living with him for nearly six weeks now, though there were days at a time when I didn't see him, thanks to his busy travel schedule. The guys were mere weeks from the playoffs and well positioned for a strong run at the Stanley Cup.

And I was busy wishing I hadn't set the boundaries between us, because I really, really, *really* wanted to have sex with Paxton.

Really.

I sighed as I stared down into my drink. It was some fizzy concoction Naomi had handed me moments after she arrived. *"You look like you need something stronger,"* she'd said. *"Or someone stronger."* I sighed as I sipped in an effort to combat my embarrassment. My mind drifted yet again to the other evening.

Paxton had come home earlier than expected and caught me watching *Magic Mike.* I'm sure my cheeks had been flushed, as I'd been considering having Paxton recreate those moves for me.

"What are you watching?" he'd asked.

"A movie you won't like. I'll turn it off—"

Channing Tatum's epic dance scene in the workshop had started as I spoke, so I dove for the remote. In my fumbling haste, I'd missed it, knocking it to the floor.

When I'd finally located it and raised it toward the TV, Paxton had gently extricated it from my hand. His touch had sizzled up my arm, causing my lips to tingle and my nipples to harden as I yearned for his touch. I'd had to shift my thighs, pressing them together in an effort to ease the ache between them.

"*This is what you watch when I'm not here?*" he'd asked, seeming amused.

"*No! Well, tonight, sure, because it was on…*" I'd searched for it on his streaming services, desperate for a release of the sexual tension that had bloomed with such intensity between us.

"*He's got some sweet moves,*" Paxton had noted as he tilted his head and squinted. "*It's like he's made of oil.*"

I'd groaned as I flopped back against the couch and stared up at the ceiling, willing the movie to end so my embarrassment could, too.

Paxton had shifted on the couch, stretching out his long legs, his thick thigh pressed against my much smaller one. I hadn't been able to pay much attention to the remainder of the movie because I'd been so focused on where Paxton and I touched… And I'd daydreamed about how I would touch him.

Yet even then, my fear of him leaving me after we had sex held me back. It was irrational. Ridiculous. I'd known it then, and I knew it now, days later.

He'd done nothing to make me think he would. And yet… yet…like Eurydice in *Hadestown,* the Fates whispered in my ear, telling me the wind would change, and I would be thrust out into the cold once more.

Bereft.

I hated those voices, had tried to silence them.

I had failed for weeks, and I'd become enraged with myself for my paralysis. So, a week ago, I'd asked Ida Jane, a children's counselor, to recommend someone for me to talk to. She'd given me three names, and I'd connected with a therapist. We'd had our first session earlier today, and we'd delved into my past and my fears. I couldn't tell if talking was helping, but it was totally exhausting. That allowed my mind to wander back, once again, to the night Paxton and I had watched *Magic Mike*.

Another dance scene had flitted across the television screen, and Paxton had leaned forward so his elbows were on his knees.

"*Guy has talent,*" he'd muttered. "*I can see why the lady likes him.*"

"*It's more than just his moves…*" I'd begun. "*But, yeah, he's sexy.*" I'd pressed my lips together, wondering why I'd said that.

Paxton hadn't responded. When the movie ended, I had turned to face him. He'd appeared melancholy for a moment before he'd schooled his features. "*If I were a woman, I think I would have been totally turned on by that,*" he'd said.

"*That's the point,*" I'd agreed. After chewing my lip until it hurt, I'd blurted, "*I want you, badly. I mean sexually. But I have this… block. Almost a phobia. I'm scared if we're together, I'll end up hurt, back in the hospital… It's ridiculous, I know, but it feels so real…*"

Paxton had embraced me tightly, as if he could hug the fear from me. If only. "*I didn't realize that was an issue,*" he'd said.

"*I…didn't want it to be.*" I'd lifted my head to look at him. "*I've been working on it, trying to get over it, but I think I need professional help—*"

He'd nodded. "*Ah, Hana. If there's one thing I've realized, it's that those emotions, especially fear, are much stronger than logic.*" He'd kissed the crown of my head and slowly, I had relaxed against him, melting into his warmth. "*I don't ever want you to have to hide from me. Not your thoughts or your feelings. I've missed our ability to be close…*" His voice had cracked, and he'd cleared his throat. "*I've missed us, Hana. So if you need more time, that I can give you. Weeks, months are going to pass no matter what. At least now I get to share them with you.*"

"What do you think, Hana?" Keelie asked, her pretty eyes sparkling as she smiled at me, yanking me from my memory.

"I wasn't paying attention," I admitted.

"Lost in Naese-land." Naomi laughed.

I wished. I needed to get over my hang-up and jump him already. Because I had to face reality: Paxton was a young, healthy male. He worked hard, and he'd always played hard. He deserved a woman who did the same with him and for him.

"Have you been worried about that?" Ida Jane asked from my other side.

My cheeks blossomed hot as I realized I'd said that aloud. But I nodded. These women had proven to be great friends. And I needed to talk.

"Let's have it," Ida Jane said as she caught my cold fingers and gave them a squeeze. "What's your worst fear?"

I puffed out a breath. "That he'll leave, and I'll be hurt—physically as well as emotionally. Maybe I'll lose my leg, like I should have before. Not be able to walk. Not survive." I whispered the last words, hating how they weighed on me.

"After what you've been through, I think that's a pretty normal reaction," Millie said. "I mean, I ran away from Luka because my subconscious bastard of a mind expected him to be like my ex and my father. But he wasn't and he isn't, and I'm thrilled that I was brave enough to overcome the need to keep running." She shook her head. "I wasn't protecting myself, like I thought. I was hurting us both by not being open and vulnerable—by letting fear win."

Millie glanced over at Ida Jane to see if her therapist friend agreed. Ida Jane nodded, seeming thoughtful. "Fear is a real bitch," she said.

I straightened my spine. Okay, well, then I would simply *refuse* to be afraid. Not anymore. I'd stood up to Jeremy. I'd made my peace with my mother. Paxton wanted me in his life. He hadn't hurt me since we'd reconnected and didn't want to. If anything, he kept trying to coddle me. I loved that, but I probably shouldn't.

But that was beside the point. We were together at *his* request. I lived with him because *Paxton* had asked me to.

No way was Paxton going to throw me out on the street. He wasn't going to leave me again. He'd promised, and I believed him—not just because I wanted to, but because I'd noted the sincerity in his expression, and I'd seen how seriously he took the commitments he made to his teammates and their partners.

Paxton meant what he said to me. He wasn't a naïve college student any longer; he didn't blindly listen to his father. He was his own man who knew what he wanted.

And he wanted me.

I hugged myself as the warmth of that realization permeated my chest and spiraled outward. Oh, that was delicious! I wished Pax was here so I could hug him—or better yet, throw myself at him as we both wanted.

A horn blared from the TV, and I looked over to see Naese with his arms up, stick clutched in his left hand, a huge smile on his face.

"Naese's fourth hat trick this month," Paloma said. She smiled my way. "Something's going right in his life."

"He's scored three goals *again*?" Keelie asked, looking up from her diapering. "Wow. He's on fire."

"What's that sign he just made?" Naomi asked. "I've not seen him do that before."

"Oh." I put a hand to my reddening cheek as a catch hit me in the chest—thrown right at my heart. He just kept proving himself over and over again.

"You know," Paloma said. Her eyes sparkled.

My cheeks flamed even brighter. "Erm, yes. It's just… He used to do that…for me."

"Well, I can guarantee the reporters are going to want the details," Ida Jane said. "Tell us now so we don't have to wait."

"There's not much more to say. Pax started making that sign— it's an H—the first time he scored a goal back in peewee. He said it was for me."

"Aw. That's cute," Keelie said. Brooks continued to fuss. She settled with him in a chair and began to nurse.

"So, there's something that's been bothering me about the story you told us when you first showed back up on Naese's life,"

Naomi said. She was reclined in one of Paxton's huge chairs, her son, Felix, on her chest. His tiny back rose and fell under her splayed palm. "Why did Naese's dad push you two apart?"

"Because Sawyer, that rat bastard of a husband of mine, was hiding his affair with Hana's mother."

Our heads whipped toward the front door, where Rosemary Naese, Paxton's mother, now stood.

CHAPTER 22
Hana

"That's…" Keelie stared down into her cup, muttering to herself. "I hate cheaters." She looked close to tears. I didn't know her backstory, but it was clear some important man in her life had hurt her through an affair.

"Fucked up," Naomi said. She was the brashest of the women, and she didn't seem to care if she upset Mrs. Naese's sensibilities. Granted, from what Pax's mother had just dropped, I was pretty sure it was my sensibilities that were smashed.

Keelie cupped the back of her son's head and kissed his little temple before she transferred him into his car carrier.

Rosemary stepped farther into the room as she tucked a set of keys into her bag.

"He did *what*?" I asked. "Wait. How are you here?"

"I flew in. I have a key—I've never used it before. I guess I should have called first, but honestly, I couldn't think about anything but getting to you and Paxton." Tears trembled in her eyes. "You needed to know immediately."

Based on her red-rimmed eyes, I realized she'd also needed to escape Mr. Naese. I swallowed as I looked at the women surrounding us. I knew from them and from Pax that he'd told both his parents not to contact him. I also knew Rosemary was a kind, loving woman—the type of mother I'd fantasized about for years. My instinct was to comfort her, so I rose. She wrapped me in one of those big hugs I'd missed very much. I inhaled her soft, floral scent and closed my eyes. Now, finally, after so many years, I felt like I was home.

"Missed you, my sweet darling," she said against the crown of my head. "Oh, how I've missed you." Her voice warbled. "Damn the man for making me think… Well, he was wrong, and you're here. Thank goodness."

She pulled back and rested her hands on my shoulders, giving me a onceover. "You've lost weight and haven't spent enough time outside. You're here in Paxton's house while he's away, so I'm guessing you're staying here." She smiled.

I guessed that was good, but I wasn't going to budge for Pax's mother any more than I would have for Aiki or Mr. Naese. I might not be ready for total intimacy with Pax, but no one was going to push me around or decide my future for me.

"Do you have anything with alcohol?" Rosemary asked, her voice cracking.

Paloma rose and headed into the kitchen. She brought back a triple shot of the tequila she'd used in the cocktails.

"Thank you," Rosemary said before downing half the glass. She hissed and made a face. She shook her head before she returned her attention to me. "The flight attendants only gave me two tiny bottles of wine. I really needed that."

"So…" Naomi said. "You're here because…?"

Everyone crowded in closer. "To tell Hana and Paxy about his *horrible* father." Rosemary hiccupped behind her hand. She finished the drink. "What's going on with you, sweet girl?"

I shrugged. "I lost my job in California, so I moved here almost two months ago to work on a new project with NASA with one of my former professors."

"Sounds like you leveled up. And you're staying here, with Paxy?" Rosemary asked, eyebrows raised.

The liquor seemed to be hitting her system already. I wondered if she'd eaten anything—if I should offer her something. "I have been, yes. He asked me to."

She smiled brightly, her eyes shining. "That makes me ecstatic." The *sssss* sound in that word was extra long. The alcohol was definitely having an effect. "The two of you were *meant* to be together. I've been on tenterhooks waiting for Paxy-poo to come out of his funk, pull his head from his ass, and do right by you."

"In tequila, veritas," Millie said.

Ida Jane shushed her, but I agreed. At least Rosemary wasn't opposed to Paxton's relationship with me.

"Paxy-poo?" Ida Jane whispered.

I winced. Pax detested that nickname, and I knew Rosemary wouldn't have used it if she wasn't sauced.

This situation, and Paxton's privacy, could go south, quickly.

"Don't, Idge," Millie said. She peeked over the edge of the pack 'n play where Bree was sleeping. "You'll start something you can't win—even with Maxim's support. These guys make up the *worst* nicknames."

"It's true," Naomi said. "For a while one of the guys was called Tiddly because he had a small, er, package."

I bit my lip to keep from laughing at Naomi's attempt at decency. Little late for that.

"Well, that's not the worst one I've heard," Mrs. Naese said. She removed her coat and set it on a barstool. Then she grabbed a glass and poured herself a mojito. After a long sip, she smacked her lips. "It's missing the alcohol, but it'll have to do. Actually, I probably don't need any more alcohol. The room's spinning."

"I might," I muttered.

The crew of ladies abandoned the game to settle in the kitchen, no doubt desperate to hear the rest of the story Rosemary needed to tell. She motioned me over next to her. "I'll dish on the boys—I've raised three athletes, and Hugo and Devon also played hockey, so I have dirt—but first I need to give Hana some more details about the situation between our families." She peered at the ladies, who'd edged in closer still.

"I expect each of you to help me ensure Hana and Paxton get their fair shot. That'll mean a lot of support and maybe some lying to keep Paxy—er, *Paxton's* dad out of the way for a bit longer. I don't want the garbage can of a man to know I'm here. Yet. I'll slap him with my divorce decree as soon as I'm ready." She stared down in her drink and mumbled something about the best years of her life.

"Hey, now! I don't lie," Naomi said.

"No, honey, you tell it like it is, which is why you're going to lead the press charge," Rosemary said. She pointed at Millie. "You have a sweet face, so I bet you could get away with a few fibs."

"Erm…" Millie turned bright red.

"We'll work on it," Ida Jane said, sticking up for her friend.

"Great." Rosemary took another long sip of her drink before she grimaced. "Damn, that liquor's making it hard to think. Well, let's see…" She took a deep breath and let it out slowly. "There's something you and Pax don't know. That's part of why I'm here. In high school, Sawyer wanted to adopt you."

I gaped. "Wh-*what*?"

"Well, I did, too, of course. *Always.* You were my darling girl. But you clearly had a family, and I found it odd, even then, that Sawyer was interested in you. I mean, you know the man. I may love him, but his head permanently lives up his ass."

"I think you're the coolest mom I've ever met," Naomi murmured. "I want to be you. I take back all the mean thoughts I had about you when Adam told me you and your husband tried to pressure Naese into ditching Hana the second time."

Rosemary lifted her glass in salute. She wobbled a little, and the tip of her nose had turned red. "Not sure Paxy—er, *Pax* will agree with you, because I had no idea my husband was a cheating cheaty cheater. The absolute bastard. If I'd known, I would have left his butt years ago. As it is, I'm more than ready to let him take the medicine he most richly deserves."

Poor Rosemary. She'd spent decades with Sawyer Naese, and now she was in her estranged son's kitchen spilling secrets and tears with women she didn't know. This couldn't be how she'd seen her life playing out.

Supportive noises and pats came from all sides.

I blinked, shocked by the surrealism of my situation. "I don't understand…"

"I need to start at the beginning, honey," Rosemary slurred. "Problem is, I guess I don't know exactly where that is."

"Um…maybe the fact that my mother and Pax's dad were…"

uh, they were together?" I pressed my hand to my stomach, which heaved and twisted. "That's…"

"Horrifying," Keelie whimpered.

"You had no idea?" Ida Jane asked Rosemary.

"Nope, none. I mean, he was a hockey player. Never got called to the NHL, but he was good. I traveled with him until our older boys came along, and he wasn't cheating then. I know because he was in my bed every night. That came *after* Paxton's brothers." Rosemary inhaled and grimaced, staring into her empty glass. "He met your mother in Manhattan. I don't have all the details, but it wasn't a—what do you call it?" She pursed her lips as she stared into her empty glass. "It wasn't just a hookup."

The women around me shifted, likely not enjoying someone their mother's age using their slang—or the story Rosemary had to tell. They were all married to professional athletes, and they were well aware of the women throwing themselves at their partners.

"There's something seriously wrong with a culture where women try to incite cheating so they can brag about fucking a professional athlete." Naomi shook her head, a frown pulling at her thin, perfect eyebrows.

"Totally agree," Rosemary said. She faced me again, taking my hands in her trembling ones. "But this was a full-blown affair. He started making up excuses to go to New York or to scout a potential kid for the program—he's a coach for the University of New Hampshire. He did that for years, I realize now."

"What does that have to do with adopting Hana?" Paloma wanted to know.

Rosemary blinked, clearly pulling herself out of a memory—or the alcohol haze. "Right. Yes. Well, it was obvious that your mother wasn't much of one to you, and I was worried about both you and Aiki. He'd fallen into the wrong crowd. Sawyer was worried about you following down that path. We talked about it often."

It was hard not to worry. My older brother had turned sullen, then mean. I nodded as those memories washed over me.

"Well, Sawyer was very worried he'd get physical with you, and I wasn't going to let that happen." Rosemary puffed out her cheeks as she blew out a long breath. "So Sawyer and I talked to your mother." She studied me. "She never said anything?"

I shook my head, but dread had built in my belly, turning it heavy. "Yeah, actually, she did. I just didn't understand it."

"What did she say?" Keelie asked.

I sucked in a breath as my stomach pitched. *No, no, no, no, no…* That couldn't be. Paxton and I couldn't have the same… "That I sure had proven to be her meal ticket."

CHAPTER 23

Paxton

"Mom said she talked to you," I told Hana as I walked into the kitchen the next morning. Well, technically, it was the middle of the night, but I wasn't surprised to find Hana awake. My mother had been inebriated on the phone, the first time I'd heard her that way, and the story she'd told me was even more unsettling than the slur in her words.

Sleep wouldn't come for Hana either, if she felt anything like I did; I was keyed up on anger, disgust, and worry that swirled through me like a toxic stew, and I didn't like it. *What on Earth had my father done?* I set my keys on the counter before I pulled out my wallet and phone. I plugged the phone into the charger, completing my little routine.

Hana stood in the opposite corner of the kitchen, wearing an oversized sweater she'd pulled down over her hands. She looked small and dejected. "She did. I'm shocked."

"Me, too. I mean, my father and your mom didn't even seem to like each oth—"

She raised her hand, and the cuff of her sweater fell back. I was taken by the daintiness of her long fingers. She could have been a cellist or pianist—her hands seemed made for creating music. But Hana loved sump pumps and spark plugs more than strings and chords. I'd seen her work her hands deep into an engine where she'd managed to fiddle with a tiny screwdriver to make my dad's old Chevelle sing.

"None of us had even considered the possibility," Hana said. "Not your mother, definitely not me. I just... I can't believe my mother would do something so awful to your family." Her chin wobbled, and she blinked rapidly.

"Oh, Hana. This is such a mess." I sighed as I stepped nearer. I wasn't sure she was ready for my touch after this latest news, so I paused, willing her to come to me. She didn't, and the hurt cut deep.

She looked down at her feet. "Maybe this is for the best." She lifted her head and met my eyes, hers full of longing and sadness. I hated that look, and I never again wanted to be the cause of it.

"How's that?" I asked.

"Well, I just realized tonight that I can't resist you any longer." She offered a tremulous smile. "You're one of Houston's hottest bachelors, as I'm sure you know. But if you're also my—"

"Stop it, Hana. I care about you, and nothing changes that. This can't be true." Unable to resist any longer, I crossed to her and cupped her cheek. She nuzzled into my palm. "Just...let me be there for you," I begged, my voice cracking as emotion slammed into me again.

There was no way—*none*—that what I felt for Hana wasn't right. Beautiful. Perfect. Which meant there was no fucking way we were related. *No way.*

But I understood her comments; I'd considered them myself on the plane ride home.

"I don't want you to feel responsible for me. I'm a grown

woman. I have a degree from a great school, and a really excellent career with NASA." Her lips twisted. "And if I'm terribly unlucky, I've expanded my family to include you."

"I want to be your family, Hana. I always have, but not like this."

"No." She scrubbed her palms across her face. "Not like this. Maybe this explains why there was such a gulf between Mother and me."

"And if it does?" I asked.

"I'm just so…*sad*." She leaned toward me a little, and I took it as a cue to wrap her in my arms. Holding Hana was right. "And angry. I'm really angry, Pax, that our parents made us something dirty." She shuddered as she shoved her nose into my sternum.

"Me, too. I should have realized…"

"What?" Hana asked.

I loved that she could still read me. Knowing that she still understood me lessened some of the ache in my chest.

"That my father was a selfish, weak asshole who only looked out for himself. His wanting to break us up, leaning hard on me—it all makes sense. It was to cover his cheating, his lies, so he didn't have to live with the consequences of his actions."

Hana rested her cheek against my chest. "Yeah, you're right."

We held each other, and my heart ached at the thought of never being able to do this again. We teetered on the edge of something horrific, something that would utterly destroy our understanding of self and our connection. But it couldn't be true. I swallowed the panic that clawed at my chest and up my throat. Just because Mei Sato said something didn't make it true. We needed a genetic test, and we'd get one as soon as the facility opened in the morning. I knew this because both Coach Whittaker and Gunnar Evaldson had promised me after I'd finished the conversation with my mother and poured everything out to them on the plane. Those men never broke their promises.

Unlike my father.

My lips twisted. Just mine. Not Hana's.

"I don't get why my mother moved us in down the street from you," Hana said, lifting her head so she could meet my eyes. "She had to have known about your mom, your family."

I hesitated. "I think she did. And I think that's why she did it."

Hana pressed her cheek against my chest. "Your mother told you about my mom's meal-ticket comment?"

"She did." My stomach lurched again. I didn't like the direction that comment pointed. "Which is why I demanded that my father fly out here. Much as I don't want to see him, we need to get this situation resolved, and he's the only one who can answer my questions."

Hana tipped her head back to look at me. "Do you think…"

"Right now, I don't know what to think," I said.

"Yeah, me either. But I feel kind of…" She trailed off.

"Weird? Possibly dirty? Because that's how I'm feeling."

Hana's tongue peeped out from between her teeth, and I couldn't help my reaction—my desire for her. But what if Hana and I… *No*. I wasn't going there. I wouldn't believe it. Couldn't.

I cleared my throat. "The guys all know. They're coming over in the morning."

She nodded. "I know. We have a group text."

I smiled, warmed by how accepting my friends' wives had been to Hana. We stayed connected and silent, soaking in the comfort the other offered. "How are you doing?" I asked finally.

"I'm confused and tired, Pax. I'm just…" Her chin trembled, and she bit her lip.

"I've got you, Hana. I'll be here for you." I rubbed her back and rested my cheek against her hair. She felt fantastic in my arms. *So right.* There was no possible way she was anything other than the love of my life. My dad would not take that from me. But my muscles tensed as the possibilities leaped and sped through my mind. "No matter what happens, you're such an important part of my life."

"Yeah, because we're family, right? I mean, no matter how we splice it…" Her face crumpled, and her eyes filled with tears. "We're family."

"You're *more* than family, Hana. My father's family, and he sucks."

She released a watery chuckle, but it was half-hearted. I understood. At least she stayed in my arms. I needed this—needed her. My heart ached at the possibility that we couldn't be us.

Damn my father to hell.

"If I *am* our parents' child, that would make any child of ours too closely related. Maybe that's why I miscarried. I mean, that makes sense…"

As much as I'd wanted to talk to her about the baby, this wasn't the context for it. We needed to deal with that loss, but not now. Not intermixed with the shock of this news. "Hana," I said, my voice rising as she gave words to my gravest fear. "It's not true. Stop it."

Hana slipped from my arms and moved across the kitchen. Heat flowed through me. I was possibly angrier than I'd ever been.

"It's possible. Probable, even, based on when they were having an affair."

"Don't go searching for trouble," I said.

Her jaw was set, and her eyes blazed as she glared at me. She was beautiful. I loved her fire, though I didn't love her anger and hurt and frustration pointed toward me.

"I'm sorry," I said, but my hands still fisted at my sides. Like a fool, I blurted, "I can't believe you could ever consider us as anything other than what we were—what we should be—a couple!"

"I can't believe you listened to your lying father instead of talking to me!" she yelled.

And it hit me, then, the full weight of every single one of my father's machinations. At his urging, I'd broken Hana's heart and disrespected our love *for random hookups.* Just like my piece of shit, lying, scumbag of a father. I shuddered as that reality crashed over me. Could this night get any worse?

"I'm not in a good headspace," Hana muttered. She turned on her heel, stumbling as her left leg gave out. But she righted herself quickly and fled.

I stood there, my heart ripped to shreds as Hana's words reverberated through my mind. I dropped my forearms to the counter and let my head follow. I closed my eyes and groaned.

"Well, that was tense in what has turned out to be a really tense twenty-four hours," my mother said as she walked in from the hallway. She studied me for a long moment. "How are you holding up?"

I blew out a breath and stared up at the ceiling. "I'm really angry. At Dad, of course. At you for going along with him and his lies. At myself. Even at Hana for believing we could be…" *Nope. I still can't say the words.* I would not believe them.

But I understood why she'd snapped at me. We were at a breaking point. Our relationship wouldn't be the same, not that it had been sturdy enough to withstand such a seismic explosion anyway. When I'd chosen to reach out again, I never could have fathomed the possibility of Hana being my half-sister…

I should have left her alone. We were all in so much agony because I'd wanted another shot with her. I shuddered and stifled yet another gag, as I'd done periodically since my mother had called me earlier. Hours later, I was beyond exhausted. My body ached from the pounding it had taken during the game, but it was my mind that refused to calm.

There was *no possible way*… Yet my dad had been sure enough about his relationship to Hana to force us apart.

"I'm sorry, Pax," my mother said.

"This is a nightmare," I rasped.

"It's…not good," my mother said. "I'm fairly sure Hana isn't… Never mind. We need facts." She cleared her throat and straightened. "Paloma said that was something either her husband or the team owner could facilitate."

"Yeah, Gunnar and Millie—that's Stolly's wife—are on the hospital board. They don't like to pull strings, but they've already done so for us. We're headed to the lab as soon as it opens tomorrow."

"You should probably tell Hana that," Mom said.

"I know," Hana said, coming around the corner of the staircase. Her nose was red, her voice clogged with tears. She lifted her phone. "Group text."

"When does Dad get in?" I asked.

Mom shrugged. "I'm not currently speaking to him, but I told your brothers to march him onto that plane, no matter how much of a fight he put up."

"Great." I scrubbed my palms across the back of my neck, wishing I could ease the tension there. "They're coming, too?"

"We're a family in crisis," Mom said. "We need to be together."

"About as much as I want a root canal," I muttered.

The three of us stood in the faint light, uncomfortable yet tethered together in this strange web of deceit.

"You really had no clue he was having an affair?" I blurted into the deepening and uncomfortable silence.

Mom shook her head, her lips tucked in tight. She seemed more aged than ever. "I thought we were happy."

I stood frozen in place as my mother broke down in tears. Hana went to her and wrapped her in her arms. "It's not her fault, Paxton," she said in that soft, sweet voice. "It's *his.*" She pursed her lips. "And my mother's, of course."

I swallowed my irritation and jerked a nod. She was right, but that didn't mean I sought criticism. Now I wasn't sure I'd ever get the chance to fully show her that, through everything, my heart had remained true in its love for her.

At eight a.m. on the dot, Hana and I sat side by side in the waiting room of the genetic testing facility, holding hands. Luka and Millie Stol, Gunnar Evaldson, Silas and Paloma Whittaker, Cormac and Keelie, Maxim and Ida Jane, and Cruz milled about.

My mother had chosen not to come with us, which was probably for the best. I was still really angry, and I worried what my reaction to more information would be. I refused to believe the universe could be that cruel. Hana and I had overcome our families' bid to rip us apart, a life-altering car accident, Jeremy's attempts to disrupt her life, and the years apart that made our connection difficult now.

No, we weren't going to find out we were related, too. I just couldn't process the possibility.

"What's with these older men and not being faithful?" Ida Jane said as she slammed back into the seat next to Hana.

"Terrible role models," Cruz muttered.

"Hey!" Coach said. "I resent that."

"Well, you're not an old guy," Hana said.

Coach smiled at her. "I really like you."

"It's people Gunnar's age and up that we have to worry about." Cormac snickered.

"I'm fifty-one," Gunnar said, narrowing his artic eyes and sizzling Cormac with a glare. "And I don't fuck around."

Now that I thought about it, I'd never seen his name connected to a woman's. Maybe he liked dudes—he had been very committed to having the team include all types of partnerships. Well, if he liked men, good for him. I was all for loving the one you wanted, and for me that was Hana.

I went back to my loop about the universe.

"Did we miss the reveal?" Naomi asked as she sprinted into the room.

"Are you banging your sister?" Adam asked, appearing behind her with his son, Felix, strapped to his chest.

Naomi stopped and spun around, arms akimbo. "He is not. That's a terrible question, and I'm very angry with you, Adam Kramer, for suggesting such a thing."

Adam hung his head. "I didn't mean it like that…"

Everyone laughed, and the tension burst, oozing from the room. It left a vacuum behind that was worse.

"Mr. Naese? Ms. Sato? We have your results," Dr. Fortescue said, appearing in the doorway with a sheet of paper.

"Well?" Ida Jane demanded.

"The suspense is horrible." Gunnar groaned.

"I need to know, but I can't bear it if the outcome isn't a happy ending," Millie said. Her eyes welled with tears.

Cormac shook out his hands, and Coach cracked his neck.

"Did you want to come back so we can discuss the situation?" Dr. Fortescue asked.

"Don't you dare leave us hanging," Cruz growled.

I glanced over at Hana. She squeezed our twined fingers. "Here. Now. In front of our *family*," she said.

I smiled at her.

"Right. Well, you're not related," Dr. Fortescue said.

The cheer that went up pounded through my mind. Baby Felix woke with a start and began to cry. Adam patted his little butt even as he grinned at me. "Awesome!" he crowed.

"But I thought you might want to know that you are both

related to Aiki Sato," Dr. Fortescue said. "Ms. Sato and Aiki Sato share maternal DNA while Mr. Naese and Aiki Sato share DNA with their—"

"Paternal parent," I said, grinning. "Serves my father right, getting a convicted felon for a son instead of a brilliant, beautiful daughter."

Hana bit her lip. "I should be mad at you for saying that about my brother—"

"*Our* brother apparently," I said, grimacing. I didn't want to be related to Aiki. He'd always been a dick. "You know, I can see it." I pursed my lips. "They're both assholes. Neither one of them takes responsibility for their actions."

"Stop!" Hana said, but her lips trembled as she suppressed her laugh.

"What?" I couldn't stop smiling. "I'm just pointing out—"

"That you get to keep banging the love of your life—hey!" Adam huffed when Naomi poked him in his ribs. "He was and will."

"Such a romantic." Naomi rolled her eyes.

"Well, this definitely calls for a celebration," Cormac said. "We have cake. Meet us at Naese's place for the party."

"What were you going to do if they were related?" Stolly asked.

"Eat cake and break out the Jack Daniels," Keelie said.

"Aren't we going to do that now?" Cruz asked.

"Yeah, but *happily*," Cormac said.

"Makes sense," Coach said. He glanced over at Paloma. "We're in, minus the Jack Daniels. We have to pick up Trix from school later today."

"I have some work back at the office to complete," Gunnar said as he rose. He buttoned his suit jacket before offering me his hand. "Congratulations on the brother, and on not being related to this lovely woman."

"Thanks." I shook his hand.

"We'll swing by the store and grab some mocktail fixings," Naomi said.

"And collect Ashley," Adam said. "He can play driver in case we celebrate too hard."

Naomi shook her head. "That means you plan on getting sauced."

"Ashley can handle us a bit tipsy. He can handle pretty much anything—he's a manny," Adam said with supreme confidence in his son's caregiver. "Plus, it's not every day one of your BFFs finds out he's not related to the woman of his dreams."

"Oooh," the ladies sighed, clearly pleased with Adam's answer.

"Let's celebrate!" Stol cried.

The laboratory's staff seemed relieved as our group tromped out of the facility. Cormac shot me a glance, and I gave him a nod. Oh yes, my big plans were still in play. Now for the reason I'd intended: to seduce Hana into marrying me.

No way was I waiting any longer to link her to me—as my wife, the exact place she should have been for the last three years.

CHAPTER 24
Hana

I sat on the couch in my spot in Paxton's—our—living room, totally sauced and grinning. Paxton and I shared family, but we were not related. I gulped as I realized, once again, now close I'd come to losing Paxton the way I'd always wanted him: as my lover. My partner. If that test had reached different results, I would have lost this chance Paxton had given us.

And I'd almost lost it anyway because of the fear that he'd hurt me again—because I'd conflated physical pain with emotional pain, and it was hard to let that go. But I wanted what these amazing women I'd met had with their partners. I wanted to receive what Pax was offering me. Desperately. And that yearning was finally stronger than the fear.

Keelie sprawled next to me like a starfish, seemingly boneless. "I can't handle all this drama," she muttered. "Y'all are too much. I thought my daddy leaving us for another family was bad, but Naese's father fathering your brother? *Gross!*"

"You know, sharing a brother is awesome," I said. "I plan to get to know him again, now that he's clean."

"He's in prison, Hana."

"I know. But I want a relationship with him, I think. But we've decided Paxton's father needs to step up—actually be a dad to Aiki. That's not something he's had since he was small."

"Maybe that'll help Aiki stay sober and find purpose," she said.

I shrugged. "Maybe. But I know I need to be a better sister, no matter what Sawyer does. Aiki's been mean and lashed out, but at least now I can kind of understand why."

"Nothing gave him the right to endanger people's lives." Scrunching her nose, Keelie reached for her glass and downed the dregs of her drink. With a sigh and a smack of her lips she rose unsteadily and headed toward the kitchen. "These are way better than mocktails," she said with a faint hiccup.

Cormac intercepted and tucked her under his protective arm. *Good call.* She was plastered. But then again, so was I. At least I thought I was. I'd never been drunk before, but this light-headed feeling—almost floating—was delicious. I giggled.

Paxton plopped down next to me, and I blinked up at him. He grinned indulgently. "You look shattered."

"I am. But in the best way, Pax."

"Yeah?"

I nodded, and my mind seemed to continue rolling. *Weird.* I struggled but managed to refocus on Paxton's face. He stared at me intently, waiting. *Oh, right!* "I was terrified you'd hurt me, but you haven't. You won't. My mind made up those scenarios because I thought I should protect myself." I touched his cheek. "I don't need to. You keep telling me you love me, showing me you love me, and I know you do. You've proven it often." I inhaled. "I'm not going to be afraid anymore, Paxton. I know what's on the line, and our happiness matters."

His eyes lit up, and a smile bloomed across his face. "You matter, Hana. Your happiness."

I blinked, and my eyelids tried to glue together. I shook my head. *What are we talking about?* "So does yours, Pax. We deserve a future. A happy one, now that the way ahead is clear."

He wrapped his arm around me and gently folded me closer to his large, warm body. But something was weird. Finally, the strangeness dawned on me.

"I can't feel my lips," I said against his neck.

"Not even if I do this?" he asked as he kissed me.

"Mmm... I like that," I mumbled against his mouth.

"Me, too," he said.

"And, yes, I can feel that, but maybe you should kiss my neck to see if that's numb."

Paxton's smile grew, and I knew he liked this game. I wasn't an exhibitionist, normally—but the cocktails Ida Jane and Paloma had made had eased my usual inhibitions. Paxton trailed his lips from the corner of my mouth across my cheek, leaving a trail of fire in their wake. I shivered and bit my lip to keep from moaning aloud. Paxton's dark chuckle caused another shiver to race along my spine and build a deep heat in my belly. My hands found his shoulders as my world began to spin.

He nipped my earlobe, eliciting a gasp as pleasure exploded through my body, shooting outward from my fingertips.

"I think we need to get a drink or two into you some other time," he said against my throat. "We'll find a limit where you're not so close to unconsciousness. Because, Hana, the little sounds you're making and the way you're rubbing yourself all over me has me so hard for you."

"Do something about it." I gasped.

He kissed his way back up my neck and jawline to my lips, where he pressed a chaste peck. "Not a chance. Like I said, you're plastered. And I've waited this long to make you mine again. I'm more than willing to wait another day—but I'm not saying it won't be hard."

I giggled until I realized what he'd said, and then I pouted, which caused Paxton to chuckle as he flicked my lower lip. My lids felt heavy as I stared up into his beautiful eyes. He wrapped an arm around my shoulders and kissed the top of my head as his thighs flexed. "I love you. So very much."

I nuzzled into his chest and mumbled how much I loved him, too.

I woke with a groan. My pounding head was immediately eclipsed by nausea, and I barely fell out of the bed in a tangle of sheets in time to crawl to the bathroom and regurgitate last night's festivities.

After what had to be years of lying limply against the toilet, I managed to haul my aching body upward and into the shower.

Once there I frowned, surprised by how quiet the house was. Where was Pax? I'd expected him to snuggle me all night. The fact that I was now handling my first hangover alone caused my heart to throb along with my head.

After I showered and there was still no sign of Paxton, I dressed in soft clothes that didn't annoy my hypersensitive skin. Brushing my hair and teeth were a torture of hypersensitivity, and I stumbled out of our bedroom in a haze of annoyance and vague illness.

"Morning," Naomi said cheerily.

"I hate you," I informed her.

"You, Keelie, and Ida Jane." She pointed to a blanket-clad bundle with blond hair poking out the top at the other end of the couch. "You three and Paloma hit the booze pretty hard."

"Where is Paloma?"

"She went home with Coach, but I have a feeling she's not fairing much better than you this morning."

"Where's Paxton?" I asked.

"The guys went to the rink. You know, to *practice*. Because they play hockey for a living and are deep in the playoffs."

"Snark less," Ida Jane mumbled. "It's making my head hurt more."

"Yes, darling," Naomi sang. I winced. She cackled.

"I want to go to the rink," I said.

Ida Jane peeked out over the top of her blanket. Her eyes were bloodshot, and her face was pallid. "Why?"

"Because I need to see Pax."

Naomi rose from the couch and stretched her arms over her head. "Sure. I'll drive."

"Where are we going?" Millie asked as she popped out of the kitchen. She had a cup of steaming coffee that I would have shanked her for if I'd had the energy.

"To the arena," Naomi said. She glanced at me, then at Ida Jane. "After we get these two some painkillers, grease, and caffeine."

Ida Jane and I slumped at the breakfast bar as we ate the fried sausage and potatoes Naomi placed in front of us. "I wanted to use the range," Ida Jane said on a sigh. "But Mrs. Naese did a good job with it."

"Where is she?" I asked.

"She left about ten minutes before you got up."

"Where?" I asked.

Millie pursed her lips. "To see the lawyer I recommended. About a divorce."

I nodded. "Good. I hope she takes Mr. Naese to the cleaners."

Naomi chuckled. "Look at you, Hana! Growing some claws."

"It's the quiet ones." Ida Jane shook her head.

"Well, we never worried about that with you," Millie said, bumping her friend's shoulder.

Now that I'd had a few bites of food and the painkiller washed down with strong, black coffee, I was feeling more human.

"So, I really think we should go to the spa or shopping today," Naomi said.

"I want to go to the rink," I said again. I was stuck on the need to be near Paxton, and no amount of suggestions or cajoling would change my mind.

We collected a couple of the other partners and wives who'd come over yesterday and stayed at our place last night. I should have been embarrassed by my lack of memory, but most of them had clearly partied hard, too, so I figured my poor hostess skills would be forgiven.

The pulsing beat of Ginuwine's "Pony" blared through the stadium's speaker system as Millie, Ida Jane, Keelie, Naomi, and I made our way out toward the ice. Naomi was in the front, and she stopped so suddenly, we bonked into her.

"That can't be what they're practicing to," Millie said.

"Unless Coach has a new plan, no," Keelie said.

"The hell is going on?" I asked. I was getting better at cursing and telling people my mind. I liked this more assertive version of myself, and Paxton did, too.

"I'm glad you ladies showed up," Paloma said, joining us. "I wanted to call you, but Silas swore me to secrecy."

"What's going on?" Millie asked, pushing forward.

After a few nudges and a firm shove from Ida Jane, who was tiny even compared to me, Naomi moved and the rest of us stepped onto the rink floor.

A collective gasp sighed around us. The guys were on skates, but without their pads or gloves or helmets. They wore, well, way less than I was used to seeing them wear on the ice—as in next to nothing because those tight compression pants molded to their firm muscles.

"Holy McMoley," Ida Jane whispered. "Maxim's doing…"

Keelie fanned her face. Her eyes went glassy as she focused on her husband, who was swinging his hips even as he skated backward. "They… I never knew Cormac could move like *that*!"

It was like that crazy dream I'd had watching *Magic Mike*—the dream that merged male-stripper dance moves with hockey. And, oh my gawd, did these guys pull it off better than I'd imagined.

Millie whimpered, and Naomi whispered a few choice words about Adam's ass.

The song ended, and the guys regrouped in the middle of the ice. Cormac and Cruz each said a few words before Paxton cupped his hands and yelled, "Again!" up at the sound booth.

He turned back to the guys huddled at the far end of the ice.

"This *has* to be perfect."

"This has to be a surprise," Naomi muttered.

"It is," Paloma said, grinning.

"We shouldn't be here. They're obviously working so hard to make it—*crap*! They noticed us!" Naomi turned around, eyes wild. "Lie," she hissed. "*We saw nothing!*"

As one, the guys turned toward us as we milled around, trying to appear nonchalant.

Pax skated over, stopping just at the edge of the ice. He studied me for a moment. "We were practicing," he said.

"What for?" I asked, trying to ignore the image branded in my brain. Paxton was much better looking than the actor in the movie, and the heat in his eyes was for me. Only me.

I could get drunk all over again off of how much this man loved me. Instead, I took a steadying breath and met his lust-filled gaze with my own.

"A surprise," he said, his lips kicking up a bit. "But I think you, Miss Nosey, ruined it."

I gasped. "I did not! I just came to see you—"

His breath fanned my cheek, tickling the nerve-endings he'd sent into overdrive last night. "Because you wanted to see me?"

"Yes," I breathed.

"I *crave* you, too. Naked and staring up at me with those big, soft eyes." He pulled back enough to see me. After a moment, he leaned in close and murmured against my ear. "Just like that, though I'd be lying if I said I didn't want to be buried inside you right now."

"For the love of hockey, will you tell me what's goin' on?" Ida

Jane complained.

"And how I can get season tickets to this show?" Millie added. She sent Stolly a sultry look that I nearly missed thanks to the sensual daze I found myself in.

Stol chuckled and winked at Millie.

"Wanna see what we've been working on for you, Han?" Paxton asked. He slid his nose down my cheek. Because he was on skates, he was even taller than normal, so he was basically bent over me. I slid my hands up his warm, thick biceps to his shoulders. I hovered my lips over his and whispered, "Yes."

"Fuuuuuuck." Much to my surprise, he didn't kiss me. Instead, he pushed back, using the momentum to skate away.

"Looks like we're finished practicing," Maxim said.

"Time for the main event," Cormac called. He shot Keelie a smoldering look, and she whimpered as she gripped at my arm.

"Pull yourself together, woman," Naomi snapped.

"Can't. He's damn potent." Keelie gasped.

"No kidding," Naomi agreed. "That's why we have to show them they don't own us."

"But they do," Millie said with wide eyes.

"They really, really do," I said.

Naomi tossed her hands up. "You're right. Okay. Let's sit down. I don't think our legs will be able to withstand this level of sex appeal."

My hangover faded still further as I perched on the edge of my seat.

Whoever was manning the sound booth had a great flair for drama because they dropped the lights as the pulsing beat pummeled my ears. But it was Paxton's ability to move his body—his hips gyrating, his thick thighs and tight butt flexing as he and the guys worked through the dance routine he'd modified for skates—that really got the job done.

His stuttering hips caught my attention, and I licked my lips, but it was the fact that he'd remembered my throwaway comment—that he'd enlisted his teammates in this crazy scheme because he knew I'd find pleasure in the outcome—that pushed me from the teetering edge of love into full-blown adoration.

I'd loved Paxton since I was a child and looked into those bright, curious eyes for the first time. But now he'd become the center of my world. I'd proven I could live without him. I'd finished my degree and even found a new position I loved. I was my own person, but I wanted my destiny intertwined with Pax's. I planned to spend my days proving to him that he not only deserved my love but made me better because of his willingness to support and love me back.

The dance number ended with the guys on their knees, leaning back until their bare shoulders were against the ice. Their heavy breathing and sweat-slicked bodies showed just how hard they'd pushed themselves.

Naomi wolf whistled while Ida Jane, Keelie, Millie, and I screamed our approval.

"That was a hell of a show." Paloma stood next to me, her arms crossed.

"One they need to repeat when I'm not hungover and can really appreciate it," Ida Jane added.

"How did you know about this?" Naomi asked.

Paloma grinned. "Who you do think is running the sound and light board?"

"Coach?" We all gasped.

Paloma's delighted laugh cut off when she turned back to the ice. "Oh. Well, Hana, I don't think your show's over just yet."

We turned our attention back to the ice, and I frowned because Paxton was no longer there.

"Stand up," Paloma suggested.

Naomi, Keelie, Ida Jane, and Millie were all clutching hands. I swallowed as I rose on unsteady legs. Paxton was just inside the boards, on his knee, which is why I hadn't seen him.

On his knee...

A small box nestled in his large hand. He wasn't... My fingertips went to my lips.

"Hana, I love you," Paxton said, his voice strong.

I squeaked.

"I've always loved, and I always will love you," he continued. He was.

"I want you to be in my life, as my wife, always." His throat worked as he swallowed the emotion that poured from his beautiful eyes.

"We paid for me doubting us before—you so much more than me, and I hate that with every fiber of my being, which is why I want you to know I won't ever, *ever* doubt us again."

I couldn't speak. Too many scenarios flashed through my mind as I struggled to breathe through the shock.

Pax shifted, and I realized he must be cold, his knee achy from the hard ice. That broke me from my trance, and I shot forward, scrambling through the door so I could throw myself into his arms.

"I know it's soon," he said into my hair. "I'm not going to push you right now—"

"Push. Push *hard*," I said. I wrapped my arms tighter around his neck, practically strangling him as I used my good leg to push off the ice and wrap my thighs around his hips.

He chuckled. "No way. I'm not going to push you ever. But I will tell you that I want to marry you right now. Tomorrow. The next day—next week, next month—whenever you're ready."

"Oh…oh! How did you… We were just—I can't believe…"

He slid one hand to cradle the back of my head while the other settled under my butt. "Breathe, baby."

I leaned back as I blinked up at him. Mere months ago, I'd been tracing raindrops down a window, wishing I could disappear. But now, I held my love, my lover, the other half of my soul between my arms and legs.

"We were just grappling with the fact that we might be related!" I exclaimed.

Paxton smiled. "There is not and never will be anything relational about the way I love you, Hana." He nipped my lower lip. Electricity blossomed hot and fast between us. "What's the biologic effect about genetic sexual attraction?"

"The Westermarck Effect. But you never saw me with your mother as an infant, so it wouldn't apply."

"I love it when you talk science. Makes me hot." He kissed me. "Now, I have to point out that from the time you moved in down the street, you were in our house enough that I saw you with my mother *every* day, Hana. Enough that I would have definitely felt brotherly toward you. I never did because you're mine. My soul mate. My love. My joy."

He winked, and I appreciated that he didn't lay his happiness at my feet. I couldn't make him happy, not indefinitely, but together, we could build something that grew happiness for both of us.

I laughed. "We weren't raised as siblings, but I see your point. Though mainly I think you're just bullheaded and refused to believe it was possible." I closed my eyes as the fear and anxiety of waiting for the test results washed over me again. "Thank you for having faith in us, Pax. I needed that confidence boost." I snuggled into his warm embrace. I was home. Finally.

"I'm here for you, however you need me."

"Well…" I bit my lip, enjoying how his pupils blew wide. "I'm going to need you to show me how much you love me. I mean, if you only love me a little bit then we should probably wait to get married…"

Baiting Pax was fun. Everything about this life we were building together brought me joy. He stared at me, a stern expression crossing his face. "As soon as we get home, Hana Sato, I'm going to worship every inch of you."

I sucked in a breath. "Promise?" I whispered.

He hugged me tighter, as if he couldn't bear not to be touching me. I reveled in this connection. How I'd missed it. I'd never take it for granted, I knew. Neither would Paxton.

"Oh yes, I can promise you that," Paxton rumbled under my ear. "I'd promise you the moon, if I could."

"I don't need the moon, Pax," I said. "I need you."

"That, my beautiful Hana, you already have."

CHAPTER 25
Paxton

That evening, I settled my palms on either side of Hana, caging her against the countertop. I'd patiently waited for hours—which had seemed like years—to get her alone.

My mother had gone to her bedroom, which was good because I *had* to touch Hana *right now*. I was desperate to love her—to reconfirm our love for each other.

She stilled, a sponge in her hand, as I ran my nose along the side of her neck. "It's time."

She tossed the sponge on the counter and whirled, throwing herself against my chest. Her arms wrapped around my neck as her legs worked their way up my thighs until her center was poised over mine.

"Fuck, Han. Fuck."

I didn't have any other words. That's what she did to me— what I sought to do to her.

"We have some fantastic, caring friends, Pax, but I've been *needy* for you all day, and it was pure torture waiting for them to leave. I mean, Naomi might have raised a glass to me if I'd said I needed a quickie in the pantry, because I really, really considered it. But I wasn't sure five minutes with your dick would be enough."

I chuckled darkly against her neck, loving her dirty talk and dirty thoughts—especially since they mirrored my own. "Well, now you're mine for the night."

She shivered and pressed herself closer. All the wonderfully depraved things I craved to do to her rushed back to the forefront of my mind. Nothing was going to keep me from her now.

The doorbell rang.

"Ignore it," I said.

Hana was too busy licking and sucking on my neck to answer. The bell rang again.

I ignored it as I carried her toward the back stairs and up the steps. But when the doorbell rang a third time, Hana sighed.

"Mood killer."

I grumbled, but I couldn't disagree.

I set her down, letting her slide along my body, giving my dick a much appreciated massage on the way. We walked hand-in-hand to the door, and I opened it to find my father and two older brothers on the front step.

"Took you long enough," grumped my oldest brother, Devon.

Hana and I shared a look and a frustrated sigh. "Why are you here?" I asked.

"Um…Mom said you wanted Dad to come so you could beat in his face and ask him why he was such a douche," explained Hugo, my middle brother.

That's when I noticed how they were gripping Dad's arms, to ensure he couldn't get away.

"No one's resorting to violence," Dad said between clenched teeth. He tried, and failed, to get loose from Devon and Hugo.

Oooh, that must be driving him crazy, to be overpowered by his sons, forced to face his wrongdoings in front of the whole family.

"Nope." I closed the door in their faces and locked it. I turned to Hana and smiled. "Race you up the stairs."

"Paxton."

I growled.

"That wasn't nice."

"I don't care," I said. "My father doesn't deserve the title, and my brothers interrupted something far more important than Dad's half-assed apology."

"We can hear you," Devon called.

"It's hot out here, and there are mosquitoes," Hugo added.

"Not my problem, you bunch of lying assholes!"

"Hey, don't call me an asshole," Hugo yelled. "I held Dad in his seat! Dude's old but strong."

"Well, Mom kind of was an asshole, too," Devon argued. "I mean, she did go along with Dad all these years—"

Mom gasped from behind me, her face stricken.

I glanced back at her. "Mom's not an asshole," I yelled through the door.

"Nowhere near as big an asshole as Dad for cheating on her," Hugo replied.

"Yeah, Dad's the worst," Hugo spat. "Really lousy role modeling."

"I can hear you," Dad said.

"That's the point," Hugo said.

"You have to let them in before they start brawling on the porch," Hana whispered.

"No, I don't, and *this* is entertaining."

"Pax."

"What?"

Hana sighed as she shook her head. "Your brothers are absolutely bonkers."

I crossed my arms over my chest and leaned against the wall. "All true."

"And they're *literally* all of our family."

I stared at her, my dreams of spending the night balls-deep inside her crashing into terrible puffs of smoke. "Not all. There's still Aiki."

Hana raised an eyebrow. Mom hovered, wringing her hands but not interfering. I had to appreciate her restraint because part of me did want to punch my father.

I sighed as my attention returned to Hana. "You want me to open the door."

She shook her head. "You *need* to open the door."

She wasn't wrong, but that didn't mean I liked her pointing it out. "Is this what married life is going to be? You as my conscience?"

"You're getting married?" Hugo gushed. He slapped his palm against the glass. "Show me the ring. Our baby bro's getting married!"

"When's it going to be?" Devon asked. "Are we invited? We better be! We did you a solid bringing this asshole out here for you to pound on."

I unlocked the doors but didn't bid them enter because my casa was not their casa. Maybe I shouldn't have been angry at Devon and Hugo, but I was, because they'd helped Mom and

Dad keep Hana's accident and injury from me.

"Pax asked me earlier today," Hana said. Her shy smile beamed, making me feel ten feet tall as Devon held her hand, staring starry-eyed at the ring.

"It's beautiful," Mom said, still behind us. "Paxton did *such* a good job."

"Always knew you were going to marry her," Dad said. He looked like he'd stepped in horse manure, but he could deal.

"Yeah, I am. *Despite* you."

"It wasn't that I didn't want you happy, Paxton," my father began, trying to bluster his way out of the situation.

I stared at him, and he deflated. "What will it take to get you to leave?" I asked.

"That's no way to talk to your brothers," Hugo said.

"Some brothers you proved to be—you backed Dad when he asked you not to tell me about Hana's accident."

Devon had the decency to look ashamed. "We didn't know Dad was a cheater and a liar," he said. "He said you were too wrapped up in Hana, and…we agreed. That's on us, and I feel bad about it, but look! You two figured it out despite our meddling, so it's clearly fate."

"We should have told you," Hugo said. "I'm sorry we didn't."

"Yeah, scout's honor," Devon said, crossing his heart with his index finger.

"Again, what's it going to take to get you to leave?"

"Paxton," Mom chastised. I ignored her.

"We thought we'd take you to dinner," Devon said with a sigh.

"Don't want to go."

"Then close your door so you're not air-conditioning the neighborhood. Invite us to sit so we can hash this out," Dad said.

I shook my head. *Unbelievable.* "Why? You lied. I found out. Then, when that didn't work, you tried to make sure I wouldn't ask Hana to come to Houston. I couldn't understand why you came to that game, talking that nonsense about Hana. But it's all come out now, hasn't it? You finally had to come clean that we might be related. Thank God it's that bonehead Aiki instead. So really, I'm not impressed with any of it, and I wish you weren't related to me at all."

Dad swallowed. "I'm sorry, Paxton. I didn't think it would come to this."

"That's because you're a lying, scheming—"

Hana slid her palm against mine and leaned against my side.

I took a deep breath. "Close the damn door," I muttered. Hugo did so.

We all stared at each other.

"Want something to drink?" Hana asked.

"I could use something," Hugo said. He shot Dad a cranky glance. "We had to chase him across the damn state."

"He did a runner," Devon said cheerfully. "Shows you what we've had to overcome in the personal-fortitude department." He rubbed his hands together. "I heard Houston has good beer. I hope you have some of the local stuff." Devon owned a brewpub in our hometown and had been getting more serious about both beer and cider.

"I just want to sit quietly and not listen to Dad try to explain why he thought having an affair, especially with Mei Sato, was a good idea." Devon grimaced. "No offense, Hana, but your mother wasn't the nicest of women."

"None taken," Hana said. "She and I didn't get along. You guys got way luckier than me in the mom department."

My mother smiled at Hana, doing an expert job at ignoring my father, who was sending out *help me!* vibes. I was pretty proud of her resolve. After making him the center of her world for over thirty years, Mom was showing her strength, and I had lots of faith that Dad would rue the day he'd met Mei Sato—and not just because he'd fathered Aiki.

"Rosemary—" Dad began.

"Drinks are a good idea," Mom said. "I'll help you."

Hana squeezed my hand before she and Mom headed to the kitchen, which left me with the three men I'd looked up to my whole life.

I realized, as I studied them, that neither of my brothers nor my father was infallible. They were human. Monstrously so. But they weren't bad people, particularly my brothers. Weak, scared, pathetic at times—sure. But I was, too. Especially during the funk after Hana and I parted.

"Before you say something else that's absolutely true but a little mean, I want you to know I've already told Dad all of the mean things. I've called him lots of names for you and for Mom," Devon continued. "And I'm particularly pissed off that he's the reason we're related to that fuckup." His face was earnest as he gestured toward Dad.

"Hey! I didn't know!" Dad protested.

"You guessed, and like a jerk, you picked the good kid instead of the one who acts more like you," Hugo said. "I mean, he's probably exactly what Dad deserves in a son, really. He got really lucky in Dev and me. And Paxton's exceptional. So, Dad totally deserves Aiki."

"That's not really fair to Aiki," I countered. "I mean, he probably figured it out or was told about the affair at some point. Remember when he was little? He used to be fun. One of my best friends."

"He did," Dad said. "Figure it out, I mean."

"And you still ignored him?" Devon asked, lip curled in disgust. "Some man, some father you are."

"I was worried about losing you boys! Your mother—"

"You let a kid in need of love suffer." My stomach heaved.

Hugo pursed his lips. "We were the better option." He shrugged as if his statement made Dad's behavior acceptable.

I was really glad we lived over a thousand miles from them now—especially Dad. Being any closer would drive me bonkers. As it was, we'd have to figure out how to juggle my travel schedule and Hana's new position with NASA we ever wanted to get together.

Did I want that?

Dad looked up at me. His expression was morose. "I was wrong, and I'm really sorry."

"How sorry?" Hana asked from my side. "Because my brother deserved a lot better than he got from you." She included Devon and Hugo in her glare. "Any of you. Did you stop to think that maybe, just maybe Aiki wouldn't have turned to self-loathing and drugs if you'd shown him the kindness and love he deserved?"

I wrapped my arm around her shoulders and kissed Hana's temple. I really loved her all fired up. That passion was addictive—and hot.

"Do we have to be nice to him?" Devon whined.

"Hana's right," Hugo said. "It's Dad who sucks. Not Aiki."

"He sucks, too," Devon said. "He's in prison."

"He still our brother," Hana said, eyes narrowed. "All of us. And you will treat him as such." She turned on my father. "And you. You'd better start visiting him." She bit her lip. "I probably should, too. I…I've been so mad at him, but now… Well, maybe I can understand him better."

"We'll visit, if that's what you want," I said.

Hugo sighed. "We'll all make an effort to rehabilitate Dad's spawn."

"Speak for yourself," Devon said.

As my brothers quibbled and my father appeared lost, my mother filled glasses with ice and I cozied up with my beautiful, brilliant fiancée. She looked over at me, a question in her eyes. Did I really want to give this up? Sure it was messy—even ugly— but it was our family.

I wasn't sure I wanted *more* of our crazy, somewhat dysfunctional relatives, and I wasn't sure I was ready to forgive my father his lies and cowardice. But I wouldn't write everyone off. That was a knee-jerk reaction. I shouldn't make those. They tended not to be the smartest choices.

We'd work out our family situation on *my* terms. Well, mine and Hana's. She and I would determine what we wanted together.

"I'm sorry," Dad said again. He turned to Mom, yearning clear in his expression. "I'm so sorry."

～

"That was really awkward, but I think we handled it pretty well," Hana said as she finally shut the door and flicked the lock. It was late, and I had to be at practice early tomorrow.

"Yeah. We did. Because we're a good team, Han. Always have been."

She bit her lush lip and peeked at me from her lashes. "I wanted them to leave sooner."

"Did you now?" I asked, my tone husky.

Hana tipped her head and looked at me. "Well, what are you waiting for?"

"I don't—"

Hana's fists found her hips. "You promised to worship every inch of my body, Paxton. I expect you to keep your pledges to me. That's how I'll stay anxiety-free and trusting."

The last few words she shrieked because I'd picked her up and sped toward the stairs, which I took two at a time. After shouldering my way into the bedroom where Hana had been staying— and I planned to sleep in from now on, too—I placed her gently in the center of the king-size bed and began to unfasten her sandals. "Too many clothes," I muttered.

Hana giggled and lifted her hips, allowing me to tug her pants down her legs. Her panties, pretty, silky scraps that I loved nearly as much as I hated them for covering that pretty prize between her legs, followed.

And then I started at the arch of her right foot and kissed my way up, up, up her leg until I rubbed my nose against her pubis. Her sweet little moans and pants had me grinding my hips into the mattress, but I persevered, starting on her other leg, kissing my way over the roadmap of scars up to her center.

This time, Hana gripped my hair and shoved my face right where we both wanted it. Her moan drowned out my groan as I licked and sucked at her clit.

"Paxton!"

I smiled as I worked her over, keeping my touch light enough to make her vibrate and gasp, but not enough friction to send her over into the orgasm we both desperately wanted.

"Paxton," she growled, tugging at my hair.

I lifted my head, licking my lips. I pushed up her filmy top and pressed kisses into the soft give of her belly before making patterns with my tongue along her hipbones and up her ribs.

"Paxton!" she cried.

"What do you need, love?"

Her eyes were fierce, daring me to defy her. "I want to strip off your clothes and sit on your dick and ride us both into orgasmic bliss."

"Yes, please," I said, smiling sweetly. I rolled to my feet and reached for my jeans' snap.

Hana tutted. "I said I was going to undress you."

I let my hands fall to my sides, enjoying the thump of arousal that caught me low in the belly. Assertive Hana was *awesome*.

She pushed my shirt upward, rising on her tiptoes as she bunched the folds at my shoulders. "Off," she said.

I complied, my movements stuttering as she raked her teeth

across the hard little nub of my nipple. "I don't know how long I can—"

"You'll hold on," Hana said. She rested her cheek against my ribs, her left hand with the engagement ring, splayed across my abdomen. I loved the sparkle of the diamonds. I loved the ritual of the engagement ring that proclaimed to the world that I'd asked Hana to be mine and she'd said yes. I took a breath and released it slowly as I cupped her cheek.

"Need a condom," I gasped.

"I'm on the pill," she said.

"And you're okay with... God, Hana, now I can't stop thinking about being bare inside you." I groaned.

"Yes. I want that, too. Nothing between us." Her beautiful sherry eyes gleamed as she hovered over me.

"Never again. No secrets, No lies. No barriers."

She kissed her way up to my jaw before heading downward where she swirled her tongue around my belly button as those nimble fingers popped open my jeans. With another quick motion, she unzipped the pants, and they slithered off my hips, piling atop my sneakers. I toed those off before Hana slid her hands under my briefs. She scraped her nails lightly along my hips before shoving the material down my thighs. I hissed as my erection bounced out of its confinement, ruddy and already weeping with excitement.

Hana's warm breath hit the head, and I shifted my head back to stare up at the ceiling, needing something to ground me as she licked my shaft from root to tip, humming appreciation as if it was the best-tasting treat.

"Hana," I groaned. She suckled the sensitive tip and raised her eyes to meet mine. I slid my hands into her silky, dark hair. "You are stunning."

She swallowed a bit more of my length, and my thighs began to quiver. Since yesterday morning, when we'd gotten the genetic results, I'd been desperate to sink inside her, show her how much she meant to me—rub myself all over her so we knew we belonged to each other.

"Hana," I whispered, cradling her skull gently.

She popped off, and I bit my lip to stifle the groan. She took my hand and tugged me onto the bed where she made short work of our remaining clothes. I slid my hands up her supple back, enjoying her curves, while she crawled over, positioned herself above me, and sheathed herself on my hard dick.

"Gah! Hana! That feels *fantastic*!"

My hands settled on her hips—as much to ground myself as her. She placed her palms on my pecs and raised herself a few inches before settling back down. Over and over she went, riding us both toward that bliss. I lifted my legs to cradle her butt and give myself more leverage to meet her downstroke.

Soon we were a sweaty, sticky mess of limbs and moans. Hana's sweet gasps drove me harder, and my thighs trembled with my imminent release. My balls drew up, and I powered into her again and again, even as I reached over and rubbed her clit with my thumb.

She bowed back, mouth open, a silent scream, as she shuddered and milked my turgid shaft. I plowed into her once, twice, before my semen boiled out of my balls and up my erection, into Hana's welcoming body.

We lay together, her head on my chest, my hands spanning her shoulders and cradling her head. I stared up at the ceiling, unseeing, desperate to catch my breath.

When her cheek bunched, I smiled, loving that she was smiling against my skin, loving that we were still connected. Loving her.

"I've always loved you," I murmured.

"I know."

"I always will."

She smiled again and turned her head to kiss me. "I know."

I lifted my head and peered down at her. "You got anything else to say to that?"

She nodded. Settling her chin on her stacked hands, she said, "I think we should get married next month."

I grinned so hard my face ached, but it was a small price to pay for this level of happiness. "A June wedding, huh?"

"Yep. I always wanted to be that cliché."

"You'll be the most beautiful June bride ever. Let's do it."

"Cool. Well, that's settled." She shifted her hips and raised her eyebrows. "Think we can go again."

I rolled us, still joined, until I was over her. I pressed my still semi-hard dick back into her welcoming warmth. "Baby, I keep telling you: anything for you."

CHAPTER 26

Hana

My wedding wasn't anything like I'd expected it to be. One, it was raining and about twenty degrees cooler than it had been the day before, thanks to a massive tropical depression that had turned inward, hitting Houston dead-on. Two, I was surrounded by a million different women and babies, all of whom were part of our wedding party, because Paxton and I couldn't decide who to include or not. Thus, we'd asked all of our friends to stand with us.

At least I no longer became anxious in the rain. Nope. Houston's thunderstorms had cured me of that. Fine, it was more Paxton's cuddling during the storms that had dissipated my concerns. These days I looked forward to the weather because I knew what was coming, and that the storm would pass with me boneless and so well-pleasured I couldn't help but remain relaxed.

Three, we were getting married at the arena, which hadn't been our first choice. We'd had to switch over to it last night because our initial venue at the Johnson Space Center was surrounded by a six-inch pond. That's why building on a swamp wasn't always the best idea. But the arena could accommodate our short timeline and the entirety of the Wildcatters organization, so now it was perfect.

And, four, Paxton's dad had begged to walk me down the aisle—on his knees, hands clasped, the whole nine.

That had been out of character for Sawyer, but he wasn't the man he'd been even a few weeks ago. He'd gone to see Aiki in prison, and he'd said he planned to set up a monthly visitation schedule. He'd also said he *wasn't* planning to contest Rosemary's divorce.

All of that had showed Paxton and me that he finally understood he'd been wrong. He had a long way to go to regain our trust, and I wasn't sure he could do it, but this situation had taught me to be thankful for the people in my life. That included my brother's and soon-to-be-husband's father.

Sawyer was currently tapping his foot and shifting in his suit. "They're expecting all of you in three minutes," he said.

"We'll be ready. Plus, even if we're a couple of minutes late, Pax knows I'm marrying him today," I said, unperturbed by the chaos swirling around us.

"How are they going to corral all those kids?"

Bree ran by, laughing brightly as Brooks toddled after her. Those two were into everything. Felix would have been, too, but he was monitored by Ashley, who somehow managed to give the little boy all the freedom he needed while keeping him safe. Naomi and Adam had hit the jackpot with Ashley. I wanted someone just like him for our kids. I'd put him on notice to find me someone as special as he was, and he'd already compiled a list of would-be caretakers for us.

I loved that man almost as much as Paxton.

No, that wasn't true. I didn't love anyone as much as Paxton.

And we weren't planning to have kids any time soon anyway. My leg was getting stronger, thanks to the new gym sessions I now shared with Paxton. He'd asked the Wildcatters trainer to develop an exercise regimen for me, and I followed it zealously. I loved that I didn't always have to wear my brace anymore.

Like today. I would walk down the aisle to Paxton on my own two feet, without any support. Just like I'd hoped.

Plus, that gave Ida Jane and me more time to hang out. She and I had really clicked, and I considered her my closest friend, something that shocked us all—Ida Jane most of all. But since we were part of the only kid-free couples, it made sense that we'd spend a lot of time together. Ida Jane was on a campaign for Pax and me to get a dog like her giant bodyguard, Blade.

I hadn't told her I'd picked out a little stray from the animal shelter that Paxton and I would collect after our three-day honeymoon. We'd take a longer one once the guys' playoff run ended, hopefully with the Stanley Cup here in Houston.

But that was still a series away, and today was about Paxton and me.

"Fall in," Naomi called out.

Somehow, the chaos dissipated in five seconds, and the bridal party lined up. Sawyer whistled in shock, and I smiled. These women, my friends, could handle pretty much anything, and so could I.

They'd taught me confidence in myself, and for that, I was immensely grateful. I'd never expected such a rich, full life, but Paxton's move to Houston had created that. Perhaps I should be angry about how we'd gotten here, but I simply couldn't be, not with this amazing life.

Paxton still harbored bitterness toward his father, specifically, and Aiki. I understood and didn't push him. He'd come around and warm to them or he wouldn't, and I'd support either choice.

Keelie straightened my veil and smiled at me, which turned to a wince as Brooks tugged her earring.

"Good thing you're cute, you monster," she cooed, whisking the toddler's grabby hands away from my dress in the nick of time. "You ready?" she asked.

"Absolutely."

"I do love a confident bride." Naomi winked. "It's the lingerie, isn't it?"

"It helped." I beamed back.

Sawyer muttered something under his breath but was wise enough to keep his thoughts to himself. I didn't care if he was embarrassed or whatever. He'd made his choices with me, here, today, and with Paxton all those years before. This was our day, and Sawyer was lucky to be part of it.

Ida Jane handed me my bouquet of flowers—ones Paxton had picked for me. The guy was as sweet as pie, really. He'd spent hours researching to ensure the meanings of the blooms together were all about happiness and love. I brought the huge array of white carnations, red roses, ivy, and purple asters to my nose and inhaled the sweet scent.

God, I loved my man.

It was time to link ourselves together, because despite the odds against us, despite the pain we'd suffered to find our way back to each other, we were home.

I didn't take Sawyer's arm. That was part of the deal: I'd walk to Pax under my own power, giving myself to him freely, without reservation.

Sawyer was here to show we were willing to mend relationships, to offer second—even third—chances, but we weren't naïve enough to expect him to change. Nor did we think the situation between him and Paxton's mother would be easy to navigate. While hurt feelings were still a struggle to overcome, we'd chosen to try to find some compromise.

Paxton's stolid countenance burst into the brightest smile as soon as he saw me headed toward him, and I knew we'd made the right choice. When I reached the front, I took Paxton's large, calloused hand and squeezed. He smiled at me a little shyly, completely ignoring his father. *Yeah, not your day, dude.*

I beamed up at my husband-to-be. "I love you."

His expression turned tender. "I love you, too, my beautiful wife-to-be."

He made me feel special, powerful, beautiful. Something I'd never expected to feel again. But that's what love was: the most powerful force on earth.

Sawyer took his seat next to Paxton's mother. Devon waved at me, and I chuckled as I shook my head. That guy was growing on me.

I tried to pay attention to the officiant's words, but I kept getting caught up in Paxton's eyes, which promised to cherish me tonight and always. I shivered as I thought back to our bachelor and bachelorette parties two days before, for which the entire team and their CATS had rented out a local golf course and clubhouse. Keelie had put us all to shame in a short round of nine, and there'd been dinner, dancing, and fireworks. It was weird, a bit quirky, and so much fun. The best part was that I'd spent the evening with all of our friends and even got to hear Cruz sing.

He was as amazing as everyone had always gushed.

When it was time to recite our vows, I turned to face Paxton. "We are our family, and we will watch out for each other, put the other first. *Always.* Even when it's hard. Especially when it's hard." Paxton's gaze held mine as he told me how he'd love, honor, and cherish me for the rest of my days.

I believed him, just as I believed in us.

We exchanged rings and our first wedded kiss, during which Paxton, being Pax, slipped me some sexy tongue. I wrapped my tongue around his and sucked harder, bringing his flavor into my mouth. We both moaned, and the officiant cleared his throat.

"It's my honor to present Mr. and Mrs. Paxton Naese," he said.

"Did he just reduce Hana to Pax's wife?" Naomi blurted. "Man, you better get your eyes checked. She's a preeminent aerospace engineer who's going to save your ass from frying in a Houston street."

"He meant Mr. and Mrs. Paxton and Hana Sato-Naese," Adam soothed.

"That's better," Paxton murmured against my lips. "As long as you're mine, Han, I don't care about those details."

"Damn straight," Cormac said with a firm slap on Pax's back. "Now, break it up and keep it PG for the babies."

We all laughed as we headed together toward the buffet that had been set up in the large conference room next door by the awesome arena staff. Rain buffeted the windowpanes, and I smiled at my reflection, enjoying the bloom of color in my cheeks and the sparkle in my eyes.

After we'd eaten, Paxton leaned over and whispered, "Happy wedding. I paid off your student loans. And your medical bills."

I smiled. "I knew it! How long have you been waiting to do that?"

He smiled. "A long time. I didn't want to scare you off or make you feel manipulated."

I laughed. "Nope. I'm glad things worked out this way. I'm thrilled to be here with you."

He hugged me close, and I closed my eyes, realizing this was my dream—the one I'd given up on, the one I'd secretly yearned for. Paxton had made it all come true because he was brave enough, strong enough, to come find me again. We were surrounded by good friends and food, kept close by love and hope.

A little while later, on the makeshift dance floor, Paxton wrapped his arms around my waist and rocked me gently. "How's the leg holding up?"

"Great," I said.

"Soon you'll be able to leg press more than me. Interested in a whirl around the ice?" he asked.

"With you? Sure."

The DJ made an announcement, and Paxton led me out to the arena. I sat on the bench as I slid on white custom-made skates, which Paxton insisted on tying for me. Keelie handed me a white faux-fur wrap that covered my bare arms. Together, with most of the Wildcatters, we drifted sedately around the ice. I breathed in the faint tang through my nose and smiled.

"Thank you," I said, tipping my head back against Paxton's chest as he held me securely.

"Of course. What are you thanking me for?"

"Today. For asking me to marry you. For loving me. For not taking no for an answer when I was too scared to join you in Houston. For believing in me. For introducing me to the greatest group of women I could ever hope to know. For not laughing at my inability to skate. For making me feel beautiful despite my rather apparent flaws. For—"

Paxton's lips sealed over mine, and he kissed me with a slow thoroughness I couldn't help but melt into. And as he kissed me, he navigated us expertly around the ice.

I broke the kiss with a laugh when I heard the thick, pulsing thump of Ginuwine's well-known song.

"Now?" I asked.

"We have to perfect our performance for the fundraiser in August."

"Well, then, let's have it," I said.

I skated to the boards and off the ice to settle in a front-row seat.

"It never gets old watching them dance," Millie said with a lusty sigh. She bit her lip.

"Nope. Never," Naomi said. "As one of the oldest married women here, I can tell you it just gets better and better—like great tequila."

"True," Paloma said.

"We're a lucky bunch," Keelie murmured.

"We chose well," Ida Jane agreed. She offered us each a bottle of water and settled into the seat next to me. "I love your unconventional wedding." She smiled. "This is way more fun than a traditional reception."

"That's because you get to ogle Maxim's ass." Millie winked.

"Definitely not complaining about that," Ida Jane agreed.

"To our hot guys," I said. "And fun weddings." I raised my water bottle, and the other women tapped theirs to mine.

"Now show us your moves," Naomi shouted.

We settled back and enjoyed the show.

NOTE FROM THE AUTHOR

Dear reader, I don't have an Austen reference ready, but I *must* tell you how much I appreciate you! When I was in college (like, a million years ago), I had a professor who pointed out that entertainment competes against all lifestyle brands. That's even more true today. You can watch Netflix, Peacock, or HBO Max or listen to music on a streaming platform while in a coffee shop, scrolling on Insta or TikTok. Instead, you spent some of your precious hours reading my book! That means the world to me. Thank you for picking it up, thank you for reading, and to those who left a review, thank you, thank you, thank you!

I loved writing this book. Each time I sat down, I grumbled, but the story was just so tender and these characters so perfect for each other that I ended each session smiling.

That's the power of a good book, IMHO.

Of course, this book leads to Lennon Cruz's love story, the book I've been waiting to write! I hope you're as excited about that one as I am. Also, my beta readers asked me if Gunnar was getting a story. What do you think? Want the big boss man to find the love of his life? Then we'd really have a Wildcatters HEA. ☺

This version of ANOTHER FACE-OFF wouldn't be here without the help of six very important women, and I want to take this moment to celebrate them.

My writing group, Carol and Lenette, you're the reason this book was completed ahead of schedule. You kept me on task when I kept getting distracted by so many other shiny, new projects. I love our discussions and how you push me to write better and to be better. Thank you.

Charity—what to say? Mainly that you make it so much easier to do what I do! From the newsletter and website issues I toss your way, to the half-baked ideas I shove at you, you always manage to find the positives. Your initial thoughts on this manuscript helped me immensely (as always!). Without your insights, well, this wouldn't be the same book. I cannot thank you enough.

My beta readers, Rachel, Alyse, and Laura. Just…wow! You put so much energy and enthusiasm into this manuscript. You drew out the best parts and made them even better. You pointed out the problems so I could smooth them away. You three are absolute romance rockstars! Rachel, your enthusiasm is infections, and I smile whenever I hear from you. Thank you for being so positive and telling it like it is. Alyse, I swear I do know the difference between a defenseman and a defender, but I'm so, so glad you keep pointing it out. Getting the details correct matters, and you have a great eye for those. Laura, just…wow! You are so thoughtful in your reads. When you pointed out how I could improve Aiki's story thread, I thought, *Of course*! But did I see that before you noted it? Nope. So thank you for your time and expertise. All the thank yous!

I hope you'll remember to buy ANOTHER POWER PLAY, Cruz's book. Those sales keep my butt in my office chair, pecking away at my faded keyboard in my attempt to bring more love and joy to our world.

If you want to chat, shoot me an email, join my mailing list, or find me on Facebook or Instagram.

With much love,
Alexa